RULE 25:
DON'T FALL
FOR THE
TARGET

RULE 25:
DON'T FALL
FOR THE
TARGET

CHARLEIGH FREDERICK

WINDING ROAD STORIES

NEW YORK   LOS ANGELES

Jacket design by Rejenne Pavon
Jacket Copyright 2023 by Winding Road Stories
Interior book design by A Raven Design
ISBN#: 978-1-960724-02-1 (pbk)
ISBN#: 978-1-960724-03-8 (ebook)

Published by Winding Road Stories
www.windingroadstories.com

To the Frederick Family Vacation
every year in Phelps and Conover.
Thankfully, vacation never ends how this book does.

RULE 1:

DON'T GET CAUGHT.

I only have a few more seconds until the security guard rounds the corner, catches me breaking in, and arrests me, which will lead to my parents killing me. But I can't go until I have the folder.

"Autumn, you need to get out of there now," my brother's urgent voice comes through my earpiece. "Rule one," he presses.

I count the seconds in my head, as my hands rifle through the file cabinet. I can't find the folder I was sent to get.

"Don't get caught," I whisper back to my brother the first of the twenty-four rules my family lives by.

I learned the rules before I learned my own name. Most parents would yell at their children for stealing cookies before dinner. Our parents yelled at us for getting caught stealing cookies, and then used the occurrence as a training exercise on how not to get caught in the future. These, of course, are the same parents who think sending friendly sniper fire at you is a great birthday gift, so I suppose the award for "Most Normal and Nurturing Parents" was never in the cards for them.

Despite all their training, I am about to end my first real

mission getting caught. I have at most a minute left before the guard returns.

"He just got to your floor."

I steady my breathing. I count my seconds. I have to stay put. Now thirty seconds left before the guard returns.

"You need to forget the file and get down." My brother watches the security feed from the first floor of the building. I'm relying on him to tell me where the guard is and how much time I have left. "Autumn!" The annoying shrill of his voice is persistent; I'll give him that.

"I got it," I hiss as my fingers reach the folder labeled in red, "The Fifth Family." I yank it out, its hard cover bashing up into the metal of the filing cabinet with a bang that rattles through the still air. I shove it under my armpit before closing the drawer.

"Hide!"

I slide under the large desk in the room. I was careful. The guard should have no reason to come in here and find me. I have to wait for him to move on to a different floor to patrol, and then I can sneak out.

"I've missed this," my brother's voice filters in through the earpiece again, calmer now, almost playful. "See, you can't talk, but you're the only one who can hear me, meaning I can talk as much as I want, and for once you can't tell me to shut up. What a wonderful change of pace. How is it going, my darling sister? You having fun? Did you remember to close the door to the room you're in?"

"Crap," I mutter and risk a look behind me. The door is cracked. No way the guard won't notice. The flashlight beam bounces off the hallway walls, coming closer. Only one hallway leads to the room. If I close it, I will be caught, so I return to my spot under the desk.

My brother sighs in my ear. Light cuts into the room from the guard's flashlight. "Just stay tight."

"Who's in here?" The guard's gruff voice booms behind me.

His feet pad into the room, and by the thud of his heavy foot falls, he must be a larger man. "Come out now!" he orders, fire in his words. And then he's gone with a curse as the sweet sound of a whaling alarm caresses my ears.

"Quinton, what did you do?" I whisper into the dark once the flashlight no longer poses a threat. Whatever he triggered did the trick in giving me my out, but a dropping pit in my gut tells me it isn't the smartest move. Though, with him, it never is.

"Rule four," he hisses back, his voice more serious; it comes out jagged and strained. He sounds this way every time he tries to run. He can crack a safe and a joke at the same time, but doing anything that requires physical activity, and keeping the same light humor, isn't in his skill set.

"Stay in shape," I recite back—*wait, what has he done?* "Quinton, you are third in line! If Dad ever finds out that you sent the whole security detail after you just to get them away from me—" I don't need to finish my thought, knowing he can finish the sentence with language more creative than I possess at the moment.

I bound to my feet and bolt out, leaving the door open behind me. This mission will be on the news thanks to that alarm. The trick now is making sure I'm not.

"I can get you out without being caught," Quinton assures in my ear. "Just meet me at the van. Abby is waiting."

I nod before I realize how stupid that is since he no longer has eyes on me. "Copy that. Tell your girlfriend I'm on my way."

"Are you from a cheesy movie all of a sudden?"

"Just shut up, Quinton," I say as I make it to the floor's lobby. A receptionist's desk sits opposite a line of elevators that stand single file against the wall. Over my head a large light fixture that looks like a beach ball made from tan paper and glass shards bounces the limited light in the dark space. Large pane windows, with no curtain dressings, rest behind the desk.

3

With the open design this is by far the most exposed part of the floor. If I want to make it out, the guards need something else to chase that isn't my brother or me. I press the elevator's down button, and as the doors chime open, I hit the "2" before jumping back out and bounding away to the stairs.

Keeping the folder tucked in against my body, I don't grab the handrail as I sprint down, doing my best to keep my footfalls silent. In an echoey stairwell, that is far easier said than done, but I know it's not up for debate: I will get caught if anyone hears me.

"I'm in the alley. You have a minute," Quinton says, and I slow down to silence my steps. If he's escaped, security will be after me next.

My boots land on the floor with a giant blue painted "2" next to a door leading back into the rest of the building. I'm almost out. I risk a peek through the small window in the door: two other members of the security detail stand ready, tasers out, as the elevator chimes open. I don't have time to see their surprised reactions and savor it when they discover I'm not there.

My heart pounds. It thumps in my head. The taste of blood fills my mouth from chewing the inside of my cheek—a subconscious habit of mine when I'm under pressure.

"Check the stairs!" someone yells from above me. I'm five steps to the ground floor and I leap the last few, landing with barely a sound at the ground level. I sprint out the side door and look for the flannel-red hair that can only be my brother's. He's crouched inside the van, a hand held out through its sliding door for me to take.

"You're an idiot," I say as he pulls me in, slams the door shut, and closes it before the van peels away.

Quinton gives me one of his annoying brotherly grins. "Come on, Autumn, I had that handled."

"Dad is going to kill you," I scoff as I hand him the folder.

Since Quinton is my older brother, he is placed as head on the mission, despite me being the one who went and got the darn thing. Whoever is in charge also gets the honor of delivering the goods.

Most missions aren't run by my parents directly—they don't have enough time to manage every assignment. Having a mission where delivery would be to my parents, for most agents and assassins in our organization, would be an honor. I couldn't think of a less glamorous delivery than our house. These procedures have always been done a certain way, and I learned a long time ago not to question that. The rules are there to keep us safe. The systems are in place, so no one gets hurt. And according to our parents, there's no double standards for their kids.

"Dad doesn't have to know," Quinton says with a look that screams, *don't you dare!*

"Rule thirteen?" I ask, trying to change the topic.

Rule thirteen: check the backseat. Dad let it slip they added the rule because mom once was attacked getting into her own car. Mom left the attacker dead in a ditch about four miles from where she'd parked, but the rule was added to prevent incidents like it in the future. I doubt anyone's in the backseat, but I don't want to talk about Quinton keeping secrets anymore.

"I checked the backseat, Autumn. That's kind of where we're standing. And Abby has been with the vehicle the whole time."

I look up to the front of the van at our getaway driver, Abby. I'm not sure how she joined the family, but I know it isn't by blood. Still, she is family to me. She's Scottish. I can tell by her accent, and a few comments she's let slip about her life. She's the same age as Quinton, that part she shared. She's skilled, and better at combat than me, though most people see her curvy figure and don't believe it at first. Then they take a foot to the throat and are made believers. She's one of my only friends that I'm not related to.

She must have told my family something though, or she never would have been allowed to join us, skilled or not. You don't keep secrets from my parents. Information, intel, backgrounds on operative, are often kept secret from me.

A large part of this organization's basis is trust. My parents need to trust the people they let in. Abby is closer to our family than most of the people working for us. My guess is she's either a runaway or was poached at a young age from a minor family. That's how we get a lot of people.

My family, the Alderidge family, is one of the major four syndicates that specializes professionally in what some might call "criminal activity." We never leave enough evidence to get caught, and we never fail a mission. If you are born in the family, you work for the family, and you never go against the family. With members all over the world, we have our hand in everything from elections and assassinations to bank robberies and jewelry heists. That is how it has been for hundreds of years. I, however, am praying I get stationed in Paris with my Aunt Magdalena who makes personnel files on everyone from presidents in Polynesia to your average pancake flipper in Memphis. You never know who you might need to blackmail, bribe, or break to complete a mission. You may fear Big Brother spying on you, but the person you should truly fear getting your personal information is my Aunt Magdalena.

That's the job for me, behind a desk in a safe bunker, only leaving to deliver the needed files to my family members all over the world. My father doesn't trust digital communication, so he stays put and hands the files off to someone else to deliver. As tonight proved, I'm made to create files, not steal them and run.

"Hang on, ya two!" Abby yells back to us in her thick Scottish accent as I grab ahold of one of the straps swinging overhead. Quinton hangs on, too, and even though he's also holding onto the folder, he keeps his balance better than I do. Abby sends the van careening around a corner, leaving a cat screaming in her alley shortcut as she misses both it and a dumpster by mere inches.

"Abby, do we have a tail?" Quinton stumbles up to the passenger seat, where he sits down and buckles in. I know Mother would yell at him for asking and not looking, but he's busying himself with buckling in.

"Nah," Abby says and glances back at me with a wicked grin. She loves driving fast. I don't want to know how many of her speeding tickets Dad has had to pay.

With a significant amount of difficulty, I move into the chair behind Abby that's facing sideways. We move so fast the night outside comes in quick bursts of color illuminated by the streetlights and business signs. A glint of a red truck. A flicker of green foliage. A flash of a pedestrian giving us the finger as Abby nearly runs him over.

"Maybe we should slow down a little?" I ask as a driver, cut off by Abby, lays on the horn. "If we break rule one because of a traffic cop—"

"I don't question how ya do ya job, so don't question my drivin'." Despite her answer, Abby slows down, and we blend into traffic as we merge onto the highway, headed toward upstate New York. And for home. Once we hit a steady flow of traffic, she puts the car into cruise and looks over at Quinton. "So, what's in the folder?"

Quinton shrugs. "Something Dad needs. I think it has to do with a larger mission. Intel or something. Unless 'the fifth family' means anything to either of you?"

Abby shakes her head, her eyes returning to the road.

"Maybe another family is trying to move in," I offer.

"Don't be ridiculous—there are only four elements."

"Quinton, please tell me you don't seriously think the reason there are only four major families is because there are four elements of nature."

Quinton looks back and sticks his tongue out at me. "I'm just saying it would throw off the balance. Four families, four directions, four elements. It just makes sense, Autumn."

"I say we throw off the bloody balance!" Abby laughs loudly and merges into the far lane.

"Can you seriously think of any other major group of four or five families that Dad would actually care about?" I argue.

Quinton goes silent, thank heavens, and I know I've stumped him. I might call him an idiot, but I know he's going to be an amazing leader one day. And I'll be... out of the way.

I'm glad I got this chance to do a mission with Quinton and not my parents, but every moment has made me wonder how many of these will I actually get? Our parents like to remind me that I'm going to live a separate life from my brother. I won't stick around in our territories and work with him. And part of me is okay with that. I won't get the glory, won't be the leader—I've known that since I was eight. I just hope tonight will prove I deserve to make some of my own decisions about my future—I deserve choices.

The way the families operate focus more on precise interorganizational politics than actual governmental affairs. The four majors rule, and the minor families that dot the globe like stars in the sky follow along, grateful when they receive protection from a family like mine. Or like my future husband's. In a way, I'm political royalty. And I am worthy of more than being sent away for a politically advancing marriage. I don't want my future to be set already. Part of me hopes that whatever is in that file will be a key to that want. Because it involves us, our family—and the fragile balance on which the world we live in teeters.

AUTUMN

AGE 7

"So, this was, uh, daddy said you lived here before Uncle moved in," I said as I ran the needle up and down through the white fabric, creating a flower out of pink floss thread.

Cousin Marleen was teaching me cross stitch. It wasn't hard, just up and down. I couldn't start a thread yet though. I hadn't mastered looping the end of the floss under a stitch, so it didn't come out. Marleen helped me with that, and once it was started, I was able to make rather messy pink flowers. I had wanted purple, but Marleen didn't have any purple floss thread on the island my uncle owned, and no one was going to town until tomorrow.

Marleen and I sat on the porch swing of the Gangster Island main house enjoying the lake breeze, occasional loon call, and the peace and quiet. She wasn't my real cousin, though she looked like she could be an older me from the south. Barely an adult, she was already under my father and Uncle's thumb, her family melding into mine for the property value. As a child, I knew her as being my real cousin.

"That's right." Marleen used her feet to swing us lightly, my legs not long enough to reach the wooden porch floor. "You go up my family tree far enough and you hit Shaffners. That's who built this place a long time ago. It wasn't Gangster Island until Al Capone's doctor moved in."

9

"Ouch," I winced after accidentally stabbing my finger with the needle. I dropped my cross stitch, but Marleen's reflexes were remarkable. She caught it before it hit the porch floor.

"Thank you," I said and sucked my stabbed finger, taking back the in-progress creation. *"Where does your family live now?"*

"What's with all the questions about my family?"

"Daddy talks about the different families, but I think we should all be one happy family."

"Ah." Marleen gave me a smile. *"Do you watch baseball, Autumn?"*

"A little," I said with a shrug. I ran my needle through the fabric, careful not to prick myself again.

"You know how there are minor leagues and major leagues?"

I nodded.

"Well, it's kind of true about families like ours, too. There are four major-league families, one of which your daddy oversees, and then there are all sorts of minor-league families, whose players will oftentimes get pulled up into the majors. Shaffner is from a minor-league family. Alderidge is in the major leagues."

"You got pulled up?"

Marleen nodded and her eyes went back to her own cross stitch. She used deep red and black to create a design she said I wasn't allowed to see until I was older.

"Why are there only four major families?"

Marleen smiled down at me again. *"How do I say this? Well, in the 1960s, there was a fifth, but they weren't playin' very nicely, so the members of the other four families got rid of the fifth."*

"They got rid of them?"

"That's right."

"They're all gone?" I asked, putting my needle down, now truly interested.

"I don't know. But if they ain't, then they're better than everyone thinks."

RULE 2:

DON'T GO AGAINST THE FAMILY.

A bby stops the van, and the iron gate swings open, inviting us in. After we drive through, it snaps its jaw shut after us. We have one hired hand who operates the gate manually at night as a safety precaution. Caden came to us from Russia when I was sixteen. We are the last ones expected for the night, and now that we are here, he can head to bed.

The wrought iron fence snakes around the whole property, creating a barrier between my home and the isolated woods beyond. If you listen closely, you can hear the hum of electricity snaking through the fence. Aesthetics matter to my father, but not at the cost of safety. Between the entrance gate and our home, a football field's worth of grass spans before the manor rises up to greet us. At night the lights from inside the house cast an enchanting glow on my father's rose bushes around the house's perimeter.

But there are no lights on in the house.

There should be lights on in the house.

As we roll between yards of green grass turned inky in the moonlight, the property appears more still than usual, and darker. I look over at Quinton who, despite years of training, still has the worst poker face ever. He senses something is off as well.

Often at night, people milling about cast silhouettes in the lit windows. With so many people living under one roof at our estate, we grew up around a constant flurry of movement. We average around twenty at any given time, though throughout the year it can spike up close to a hundred. It's like when you pass by a hotel, no matter the hour, someone is up, whether it's a cranky old lady with a cigarette, a traveler suffering from the change in the time zone, an aspiring artist who can't sleep, or a Romeo and Juliet type couple sneaking about. Yet, tonight, the house is dark and still.

About halfway to the property, the paved drive forks into three paths. Two loop up to the front doors—double set and wooden—creating an oval. A large fountain stands in the middle of the loop amongst the clean-cut grass. We call it the eye. Looking down from the roof, the loop looks like an eye with the fountain as an iris. The other path takes you to the back door like wing tipped eyeliner, which is where we're headed.

"Cut the headlights," Quinton says. Abby doesn't question him as she plunges the driveway into total darkness. If something is wrong, stealth is the best option.

"Could this be one of Dad's tests?" I whisper, even though, if anyone is close enough to hear my voice, they would have heard the van's sputtering.

Quinton shakes his head. "Mom would never let him test us the same day as a mission. I think either someone's here or we're abandoning base."

"Abandoning base?" I echo. Vaguely, I remember the last time we moved. I was four and it hadn't mattered much to me, but Quinton is older than me by about two years and would remember it better. He'd know the warning signs. We had moved here—it's the only home I've ever known. It's more than a base to me. My mother was always quick to remind me that we can't get attached to places, but I know she feels the same way I do. This is home. "I don't want to abandon it."

"Yeah, well, mom and dad rarely give us a choice." There's bitterness in his tone.

He's right, of course. But our parents encouraged us to raise our concerns. If both Quinton and I contested, if the problem isn't too large, maybe we can reverse this decision.

I look at the giant estate, tucked up behind the rolling lawn Dad puts so much effort into, the driveway wrapping around our Colonial-style mansion. Of course, he spends little time actually tending the property. And when he does go out, he goes to the roses first. But it's his vision, his light, his pride. He picked out only the finest of the gardeners that Aunt Magdalena vetted.

A tightness seizes my chest at the prospect of leaving my home for good. He wouldn't want to leave either. Neither of my parents would want to leave this place. So why does it look like we're running when we're powerful enough we should never have to run?

"I'd be more concerned at the thought that someone is here," Quinton adds.

"If someone is here, why would Caden open the gate?" I ask.

"Maybe Caden isn't at the commands anymore."

"Rule seven," Abby says.

"Assume nothing," Quinton and I reply in unison.

Abby's right. Assuming the worst won't help us. Abby's optimism makes it obvious she's not a blood relative. We first met her when I was eleven. They saw the talent she possessed, but they hadn't trained her like they had Quinton and me. They'd given her fast cars, the ability to grow, three meals a day and protection if she swore to step in front of a bullet for us. For their own children they gave reality. There's a difference between assuming the worst and being cautious.

"So, what's the plan?" I ask Quinton. From the look in his

13

eyes, he's already come up with several scenarios by the time Abby stops the van near the back door. My plan would be to storm the house ready for a fight, but I know my brother will disagree.

"Let me lead. If something happens, I want to be the first one in."

I roll my eyes. If Abby wasn't here, I am positive he would insist on ladies first.

Quinton ignores me and continues talking. "Rule seventeen. We know this house better than anyone." He slides the van door open and jumps out, his movements practically silent. Graceful. His feet don't make a sound. In another life I wonder if he would have been a dancer. But in this life, he's an operative set to take over a crime family. I follow him. The crunch of a leaf under my boot makes me wince as I hit the ground.

Quinton turns back and glares at me, as if the van had been silent and had gone undetected coming up the driveway, and that leaf would be the big giveaway.

He goes to the door and tries to open it. It won't budge. Typically, this door is left unlocked. No one gets past the fence without clearance, and the side door used by staff, as well as by our family, is a keyed entrance. The main doors are often used for show, or for a shorter walk if you approach the house on foot. This door should be open.

Without a backwards glance, he holds his hand out. A key would be best right now, but I didn't think to include house keys in my outfit this morning. Not wasting time, I slide two pins from my hair, placing them in his palm before slinking into the shadows in case someone is looking down from an upstairs window. Of course, they will still see the van, but we can't hide that in the shadow of the house.

"Autumn," Quinton hisses, looking down in the dark at the pins.

"Unlock the door."

"Where's your key?"

"Where's your key?" How is this on me? He has a perfectly good set of keys he left behind as well.

With a grumble my brother turns back to the door. "Got it," Quinton whispers. A key wouldn't have been much faster. We're lucky no one threw the deadbolt. The door clicks open, snapping me back to focus. He steps into the house. I follow. Abby remains in the van in case we need to make a getaway.

It's dark in the mudroom, and my shoes track dirt across the white porcelain tiles. Part of me wants to take my shoes off like I always do and leave them in line next to our parents under the hanging coats. Their shoes are here. Unless they didn't put on their regular pairs, my parents are somewhere in the house. If I had time, I could study the soles of the shoes, figure out where they were last worn and how long ago that was. We could anticipate what condition our parents may be in. But Quinton hands me back my pins, and as I shove them into my hair, he moves forward, leaving me to trail after, shoes still on.

We slink through the dark kitchen. The glass cabinet faces glare at us. It's like they're angry, like this is somehow our fault. We don't stop to examine anything here, as much as I want to, instead we move into the equally dark dining room where I pray I'm not getting mud on the red carpet my mother loves.

We reach the ballroom where sound echoes. At least it does now. When this place is filled with guests the echo vanishes, snuffed out by the warmth of a full house.

I know the only ones who can make my family flee our estate like this are the other three major crime families. And with limited communication when we're out on a mission, our parents may not have been able to get word to us before something bad happened.

We could be walking into a trap.

No one tells me anything about the criminal family politics. Quinton is set to inherit the family throne, while my parents plan to ship me off to Russia to marry a boy my age who will inherit the head of a different major family, the Daxterovs. And so, I am left out of most of the important meetings.

"What's going on?" I whisper to Quinton's back through the darkness. He flashes me a look that tells me if I don't keep my mouth shut, he'll make sure I do.

There's a clip of a footfall against the smooth stone floors, the gleam of a blade in the whisper of light from the windows. We're not alone. I jump on Quinton, tackling us both to the ground as a knife slices over my head and imbeds in the colonnade behind us. Right where Quinton's chest had been.

We get to our feet, knowing whoever threw the blade knows where we are. In an instant, Quinton draws his own blade out and scans the dark for any sign of movement. He puts a hand up and silently pulls me against the wall.

Quinton's knife catches my eye. He had gotten it for his fifth birthday and, like our mother, never leaves home without it.

"Grab the knife," Quinton hisses, his voice barely audible as he gestures to the colonnade. As I move toward the weapon, Quinton lets out a whistle, a high note, and then a low note.

"Stand down!" My mother's voice calls out in the dark. The light in the room flickers on, illuminating the sitting area off the ballroom where important guests often make deals with Father. In the light, I recognize the blade sunk a good inch into the wooden colonnade as my mother's, with its opal handle.

"Mom tried to kill us," I say in disbelief. My father joins my mother in the room; cross looks cover their faces even though they were the ones who attacked.

"My children know how to dodge a knife," my mother reasons, watching the two of us.

"Funny, I always thought it would be Dad to kill us,"

Quinton says to me, ignoring our parents, as I pull my mother's knife out. The weapon sits heavy in my hand and the smooth opal is cool to the touch.

I look at my parents. "What's going on? Where is everyone?"

My mother's hair is down, dark strands framing her face in a way I often never see. I got my blonde hair from the Alderidge side, and Quinton took after our father with his red hair. We also inherited his demeanor. Or at least I did. My mother tends to be calm and level-headed. She tends to look before she strikes. Who did she think we were? Who did she think could have been standing in her house? Nothing about this is right.

"Did you get the folder?" Father asks, his voice short. Quinton holds it up for him to see.

"Good," Mother nods. "Autumn, you need to bring the folder to your uncle. Quinton, you're coming with us to London."

"Where is everyone?" I demand again.

My parents exchange a glance I've never seen before. Fear maybe? It takes a moment before my mother talks again. She doesn't meet anyone's eyes. "We're evacuating the house. Everyone else is going to either the estate in Maine or to Milan."

"Why?" I demand.

"Autumn, your focus needs to be on your next mission," my father snaps. He never snaps. "Quinton, give her the folder."

Reluctantly, Quinton hands me back the folder that I had gotten in the first place. His gaze doesn't leave our parents.

"What's my mission?" I ask, taking the folder.

They're silent for a moment. "There's been a threat to the family," my mother says.

My heart rate quickens.

I don't have to ask how serious the threat is. It must be a dangerous threat, and very much real, to get my parents like this. My mother isn't the type to throw a knife without knowing the target. It has to be life or death. "Your job is to go to your uncle's, give him that folder, and then gain intel on the layout and security of one of the large waterfront properties on the Conover, Wisconsin side of the lake where Gangster Island is."

"Why me?" I ask. Our family is huge with plenty of people trained to case house layouts, and although I'm not next in line, I would rather help take care of this threat with Quinton and my parents than ship off to my uncle's.

"Autumn, there are three people who live in the house we need access to. A butler who is in his fifties and is highly skilled." *Highly skilled* is a phrase my dad uses for someone who kills first and asks questions later. "As well as a billionaire who is extremely cautious and leery of everyone. And there's the billionaire's son, Kato. The son is our best bet to gain entry into the house. He's seventeen just like you and has similar interests. As such, we determined you would be most likely to gain his trust and be invited into his house."

"You're joking, right?" The anger in my brother's voice zaps my irritation as he beats me to the punch. "You guys are saying that we are facing a threat, and you're sending Autumn to the Wisconsin Northwoods to flirt herself into the heart of some billionaire's son so you can steal from this guy while I'm too far away to help her?"

"She has to befriend the boy, nothing more," Father presses, with a look at me that says it better not be more.

"If you are going to take over this family, Quinton, you will have to learn to lead a separate life from your sister," Mother adds.

Quinton looks at me, and I can tell he hates this as much as I do, but we both know by now that it isn't going to change anything if we argue.

And that's when I notice my duffel bag sitting in front of the fireplace, the seams bulging, more ready for Wisconsin than I am. In my defense, my bag has had longer to process the news.

I'm leaving now—like right now. I don't even get a chance to let the idea sink in. This is why I hate fieldwork. This is why I belong in Paris with my aunt, not in Wisconsin robbing some rich guy by manipulating his son.

"When do I leave?" I don't look at my parents, but keep my eyes on my plaid bag, praying whoever packed it included some of my retro suits.

"Tonight." My father confirms my fears. I feel a little light-headed all of a sudden.

"It's just for the summer," my mother adds as if that makes it better. It is only early June. 'Just for the summer' could be three months. Whatever happened in the last few hours between Quinton and me leaving for our mission and arriving home tonight must have truly rattled my family.

"Okay," I say, my eyes still on my bag, my feet not moving. "But I will not do more than befriend him."

"Seriously?" Quinton demands, and I look at him. He looks upset I chose our parents' side over his.

"You don't question our decisions on matters like this," Mother says.

"Sorry," Quinton mutters, though he doesn't look it.

I know how hard it is for him to stand up for me, and I do appreciate it, but deep down I know that even if I don't understand why my parents are sending me to Wisconsin, they are doing it with my best interest in mind. As much as our parents preach that we'll be in charge one day, we don't get choices yet. Maybe that's clearer to me because I'm the one already arranged as political leverage. And because my mother says it to me, and not to Quinton.

"I'll see you this fall." I try to give him a smile, but I know it doesn't mask my nerves. Our parents are hiding something, and as much as I want to figure it out, my mission is in Wisconsin.

"Rule five," Quinton says and gives me a hug, a gesture rather foreign in my family.

I'm stiff for only a moment before I wrap my arms around my brother, holding him close.

I recite, "You are your most powerful weapon."

20

RULE 3:

NEVER USE YOUR REAL NAME ON A MISSION.

Gangster Island has its own private helicopter pad, and, although it's over-the-top to me, I am flown directly from my house to the island, only stopping once for fuel. I sleep for most of the flight, thank heavens, because every time I wake up all I can think about is what threat to my family could possibly be large enough to uproot my life to this degree. And why this mission? Why is this house so important right now?

Either my parents want me out of the way, and they figure a mission at my uncle's is a convenient way to keep me safe and my mind off things, or this Kato, his father, and whatever we need to get into his house for are related to my family's sudden upheaval.

I know my parents, and if I have to guess, I say it's all related.

Slinging my duffel over my shoulder, I hop down from the helicopter and make my way to where my cousin, Ashlynn, is waiting. Even in the humid summer air in the middle of the woods, her chocolate-brown hair is perfectly curled with just the right bounce and sway. Her Spanx shorts and tank top are dryer fresh and pressed to perfection, showing off her figure.

Ashlynn is thinner than me, her muscles lean unlike the bulk they add to me. Born premature, she had been a smaller, short child when we were growing up and never reached her full physical potential during adolescence. To compensate, she always wore heels like the black ones she has on her feet today that somehow don't sink into the grass. How is she not the perfect choice for a mission that involves gaining the trust of a teenage boy? Yet, for a reason unknown to me, I have been helicoptered here instead. I'm sure I have a drool stain running down my face, and I catch myself before tripping in my combat boots despite the estate's pristine and well-manicured grounds.

Ashlynn pulls her large, dark sunglasses off and balances them on top of her head. If we were a normal family, I imagine she'd be a model and a huge success while I probably would be a schoolteacher in a small town where my students would look at magazines with her on the cover. Why not send Ms. Perfect after Kato—she lives here in Wisconsin already. *I don't know.* But I do know it's not my place to question the assigned missions.

"Autumn!" my cousin gushes, a smile spreading on her face, showing off straight, bright-white teeth. *Of course.* "Welcome back to Gangster Island. How long has it been? Two years?"

"About that." I nod, and we walk together to the main house along a concrete pathway lined with flowers and decorative stones. "Are you the entire welcoming committee?"

"What do you want, Princess, a freaking parade?"

I cringe at my cousin's nickname for me. When I was seven, we had come to visit the island and I had insisted I be the princess when Ashlynn and I played together. What seven-year-old wouldn't? For reasons I never figured out, Ashlynn took that fun game and twisted it, calling me 'princess' as if I were a spoiled brat.

She walks a half step ahead of me, her heels doing little to slow her down. "You're lucky I came to say hi. If we had known sooner that you were coming, we would have rolled out the red carpet. As it is, I had to miss today's training on the mainland to be here and greet you. The others should be here in an hour or so."

"Who are the others?" Like my home, every fortress in my family has a rolling guest list, as people are moved around the globe for whatever mission comes next.

My cousin smiles at me as if I'm a child who isn't understanding a simple concept. "My father, of course, my brother Louie, Harvey and his husband—"

"Sam," I fill in. I attended their wedding. It had been a murder mystery-themed event. Harvey is the one related to the family by blood, but Sam hadn't even been a member of a minor family. He was an author from Brooklyn.

Harvey had been in New York City on a case that involved The Met, a diamond, and a woman who planned to steal the jewel. Harvey had seen Sam in the window of a coffee shop in Brooklyn while he was staking out the woman. He pretended to be a NYPD criminalist and offered tips to make a murder scene in Sam's novel more accurate and believable. It wasn't until three years later that he told Sam the truth. Two months after that, he proposed. My family hasn't been supportive of such a match. It isn't often outsiders are let in. And by the scowl on Ashlynn's face that mentality has rubbed off on her.

"Whatever." Ashlynn flips her hair over her shoulder and continues talking. "We're also hosting Marleen and her son— and now you, I guess, for some ungodly reason. The mission should have been mine, you know. I'm already here. My last assignment in Milan was a huge success. You heard about that one, right, Princess?"

"Right," I say as the main house comes into view through the trees. I know full well Ashlynn hasn't been on a real mission and wouldn't have had a solo. Uncle is overprotective of his children to a fault. If my father sent Ashlynn on a mission, Uncle would have come to our house to fight. As my father's brother, he has leeway—anyone else would've taken a bullet to the head.

The main house is three stories of stained logs, hand-crafted tongue-and-groove craftsmanship, and rustic finery. It's equal parts historic charm and modern convenience with a northwest corner bulge into a rounded turret. It's hidden in the shadows by towering pines spared when northern Wisconsin was clear-cut for the lumber to build Chicago, Milwaukee, and other Midwestern cities. Logging the island would have been difficult and prohibitively expensive in the early 20th century. The behemoth of a building is both opulent and as if it's always been part of the forest.

"Everyone is on the mainland right now?" I ask.

Ashlynn nods. "Everyone but me and you. Most of them are sparing and making the rounds through training workouts, but I think Marleen and her son are pants shopping."

"Lucky Marleen."

"Hardly. That little brat is a terror."

I look down at the folder in my hand, and I'm reminded of the day when Marleen taught me to cross stitch. That had been a peaceful day.

She had mentioned the fifth family. They were supposed to be gone, but they must not be. Somehow, they are key to all this. I just know it.

And that should fill me with dread instead of excitement. If they're back, then for once, I'm not the only one in the dark.

"You still with me, Princess?"

I look up, and Ashlynn is a good few feet in front of me. I glance back toward the dock. A pontoon glides across the lake toward the island.

Ashlynn waits for me to catch up so she won't have to yell again. "That should be Marleen," she says, looking past me.

I haven't seen Marleen in years. Soon after she taught me to cross stitch she had been sent down south for her own protection. About four or five years ago she came to my house to talk to my father. Now she's back at her home. A smile spreads across my face, and although I know I should go inside to put the folder about the fifth family somewhere safe, I run to the dock instead, my bag bouncing and hitting me in the back as I sprint down to greet her and her son.

"Is that Little Autumn?!" Marleen yells from the boat as it gets closer.

"Marleen!" I call back. I want to wave, but with both my hands full, it's not possible. I secure my duffel over my shoulder to free one hand to wave as the pontoon coasts up to the island's small pier. It's clear Marleen has docked a boat before.

"Well, ain't this just a treat," Marleen greets and hops onto the dock, tying the pontoon off before it fully stops moving. She's larger than me and envelops me when she gives me a hug. Straightening up, Marleen looks more like a small-town bohemian, than a trained operative. Two small blonde buns adorn her head, and her long skirt is at least twelve different colors. Last I heard she worked in town as an art teacher and helped build sets for the community theater. Her light southern drawl gives her away as not being native Wisconsin. "Why didn't you tell me you were comin'?"

I open my mouth to respond, but the roar of the helicopter lifting off drowns me out. Marleen's son, who can't be older than five, covers his ears with his pudgy hands. He looks rather cute, dressed like a country themed teddy bear in jean overalls and a flannel shirt. He has the thickest glasses I've ever seen, and I can't help but feel bad for the kid. I'm sure he's teased for glasses that big.

I give a small laugh as I turn back to Marleen and shout in her ear, "Didn't have time. It's good to see you, Marleen!"

Marleen lets me go and takes my bag from my shoulder. "Well, come on, let's get you settled."

Ashlynn clears her throat and crosses her arms, shifting

from foot to foot a step from the dock. "Marleen, don't you have babysitting duty? I'm the one getting Princess settled."

"Ashlynn, if it's your own kid, it ain't babysittin'." Marleen's smile doesn't waver. "You seem so put upon I figured it wouldn't hurt you none to let me take her to her room. If you really missed your cousin that much, I, of course, will step aside. Family bondin' is a very important thing, after all."

Ashlynn's face changes from annoyed to sweet as seamlessly as putting on a mask. "Well, you two have fun. I'll be inside if you need anything, Princess. Oh, and my father wishes to speak to you later this evening once he's home. I'm betting it's about that file. Don't lose it."

"Rule seven," Marleen chimes in.

Ashlynn and I both respond without missing a beat: "Assume nothing."

With an abrupt turn Ashlynn makes her way to the house, her high heels echoing an unnatural "clonk clonk" through the woods.

"It's so good to see you, Marleen," I say with a smile as her son bounds into step behind us. We make our way up the dock and to the house once Ashlynn's out of earshot.

"Is your brother here?"

I shake my head. "Just me this time. The rest of them are taking care of other business. But how about you? I heard you went down south for a bit with your son?" Not that I'm privy to the details, but I do know it was for a mission. I haven't talked to Marleen since she left. "Weren't you in Alabama?"

"It was actually..." Marleen trails off, a smile forming on her lips as she looks at me. I hate when people do that. She's closing up. Marleen must see the tightness in my jaw as she changes subjects. "What's this new mission you're here on? You know I'm always here if you need any help."

I want to tell her off for shutting me out. Instead, I take her offer. It's not her fault my parents don't trust me to know anything. "I'm actually glad I ran into you. What can you tell me about the fifth family? The one that left in the, I believe it was, the 1960s?"

Marleen stops and grabs my arm. "Why?" Her tone is accusing and urgent, as if I said something wrong.

"Uh, it's for my mission, I think."

Marleen nods. "So, the rumors are true. That's not good."

"What rumors? Marleen, what's going on?"

Marleen turns to her son. "How 'bout you run inside and try on those pants, okay? Mommy will be along in a minute." Her son shoves his massive glasses up his nose, and hurries past us. As soon as Marleen is sure he is out of earshot, she turns back to me. We're alone here. For once, maybe, someone will be open with me.

"I don't know if I should be tellin' you this," Marleen starts. "The four main families got together and, well, 'exterminated' the fifth family. This was back in the, oh it must have been the 60s or so. I think your great-grandparents or your grandpa was in charge. The four families took power in the late 1800s, with the Alderidge's being the oldest."

"We first started taking power in 1785 with the Treaty of Amity and Commerce." I paid attention in history class.

Marleen nods. "But the fifth family hadn't been around as long, only a couple decades since it rose from a minor to a major family—it didn't have a ton of names to cross off. There were two elders, both well in their sixties, as well as their two sons, a daughter, and their families. Four households. The original four families struck in one swoop, each taking a house and wiping out the fifth family in one bloody night."

"How do you know this?" I say in earnest. Intelligence of this magnitude I would deem as hush hush information. Marleen is talking softly too, her voice low as if she doesn't want the loon out on the lake to hear.

"The story spread through the minor families. A cautionary tale. Even if the major families tried to hide it."

"How'd they do it?"

"How'd who do what?"

"How did the four major families take out the fifth?"

"The Al-amins took out the two elders in their estate. The Thindrels took out the daughter and her family. And your family, the Alderidges, and the Daxterovs each took a brother. The four families killed them all."

"There were no survivors?"

Marleen looks up at the main house. "If this is part of your mission, your uncle will probably want to—"

"Marleen, please, I need to know what's going on."

Marleen's gaze returns to me. "Fearless child, be careful. You are prepared and trained to find the bear traps and avoid them, but you have never faced the bear before."

"I'll be fine, Marleen." Perhaps if everyone stopped treating me like a little kid who needs protection I would be prepared for a bear. I might want to sit behind a desk like my aunt, but that doesn't mean I don't know how to fight. I am worthy of being trusted. "Now, did anyone from the fifth family survive?"

"Look, it's all just rumors and speculation. Any member of the main four families will say it ain't true, but to some of the minor families, the fifth family is like the Romanovs to Russia, everyone wishing the grand duchess Anastasia made it out alive." Marleen gets even quieter, and I have to lean closer to hear her. If the four families say it's not true, Marleen disclosing it to me could be viewed as disloyalty. "The Savino family lived near one of the brothers' houses, the brother the Alderidge family was responsible for takin' out. The Savino family claims they saw a bloodied child running from the direction of the brother's house."

"The Savino family is known to do whatever they can to stir the pot. It's why they'll never be a major family."

"And yet, there was fear that the four could then take out any minor family they didn't like. If they could do it to a major family, what stops them from doing it to a minor?"

I want to open the folder in my hands now, but I know

that's not the protocol. I know it's to be delivered to my uncle, and what he chooses to share is up to him. Instead, I ask, "Who was the child?"

"One of the brothers' daughters. The rumor is she was shot, faked being dead, and was buried in a shallow grave with the rest of her family. After your family left, the story goes that she dug her way out, stopped the bleedin' in her shoulder with shreds of her dead family members' clothes, and ran."

I give a reluctant nod, my stomach turning at the gruesome thought. "Marleen, if she was shot, she would have needed medical help. Upon hearing the rumors, my family would have made sure to check the local hospitals."

"Your family did their due diligence. She never went to a hospital, just vanished. That's if she's still alive."

"So, she could still be out there?"

"I don't know. I figure that if the fifth family is tied to a mission, someone must have survived. That girl would be my best guess."

"Except the house I'm supposed to infiltrate doesn't have any female occupants."

Marleen shrugs her shoulders. "Then I suggest you focus on what you were sent to do, yeah? It's just rumors anyway."

AUTUMN

AGE 8

I ran my hand over the manilla envelope, the surface smooth
beneath my touch. With a single finger, I traced the name on the
cover: "Ballina Savino." I brushed my hair behind my ears and flipped
it open for a good look. I stumbled back in shock, bumping into the
large oak bookcase behind me before falling to the floor.

My father, no doubt hearing the noise, crashed into the office with a
sword in hand. His face relaxed at the sight of the open folder and me
on the floor. He slid the weapon back into its scabbard on his belt. "We
don't open things that don't belong to us, sweetheart." Father took off
his sword belt and set it on the desk. He grabbed the folder and sat on
the floor next to me.

"That's a bad folder," I muttered, moving close to him.

"The folder isn't bad. The actions that led this folder to be sent to
me are bad, though. You know the game you play with Quinton, where
you study a room and then figure out how someone died? It's kind of
like that."

"No," I insisted. "There are no bodies in the game."

"Because the one you play now is for children. I think you're almost
ready for the real game, no? You, my sweetheart, do not have as many
years of training as your brother. It's a crime of age and a fact that will

31

hopefully always remain true. Yet, you, Autumn, are better at observing than your brother. It drives your mother mad."

I nodded, though I couldn't recall ever actually seeing my mother mad. "She says it's going to get him killed."

"Ballina Savino didn't notice things were out of place until it was too late. That's what got her killed. This is a case from the 1960s. It's come back to my attention because DNA has finally caught up, and the person who matches was supposed to have died a week before Ballina died."

"Is Quinton going to die like her? Since he's not as good at observing?"

Father laughed. "No. He's leagues above where he should be for his stage in training. He's doing really well."

"But you just said—"

"You're still better. At this. This one time." Father opened the folder. "I'm going to show you this again. You know what's there now. Study the picture like you would in the game you play with Quinton and tell me what you see."

The folder slid into my small lap, and my breath hitched in my throat at the sight of the mangled body. But I would not let Father down. "She was killed by someone smaller than her. They relied on... they relied on swinging from the chandelier. It's bent like something hung from it. Like someone. But they could have set it up since Ballina lived alone. I don't think she got in the way. Whoever attacked wanted to kill Ballina." A slight pause, and then I continued. "The pillow is ripped open, and it looks like a knife slash. But there's no knife in the photo, so the killer probably took it with them. And Ballina is missing a bracelet."

"A bracelet?" Father took the folder back, and I smiled. I had hit a fact he hadn't seen.

"Her wrist, see?" I pointed to Ballina's left wrist where a crease indented her skin. "If it had been off her for long, the mark would be gone."

Father nodded and passed me back the folder. "What else do you see?"

The office door opened before I could answer, and we both looked up to see my mother staring at us. "What are you two doing?"

"I'm helping Daddy!" I said with a smile.

Mother spotted the manilla envelope in my small hands. She crossed the office, taking it from me and hitting my father over the head with it. "What are you thinking? Why would you show her this?"

"She was helping, she noticed—"

"I don't care if she just solved the biggest crime of the century. She is a child, and this is not appropriate to show her." Mother's voice was calm and level, even as she scolded.

"You've already arranged her marriage for her when she grows up; I think she can look at a few dead bodies."

"That is completely different. She is eight years old."

RULE 4:

STAY IN SHAPE.

The rest of the family returns to Gangster Island after dark. Marleen and her son are in bed. Ashlynn and I sit in the living room. I watch television, some nighttime drama I've never seen before with a rugged guy wooing a blonde nurse. Ashlynn sharpens her knife collection. The bear's head over the mantle stares down at us; its dead eyes only seem to bother me.

"Well, that was fun," Uncle says as he swings open the door, the rest of the party close behind.

My cousin Louie, Ashlynn's little brother, makes eye contact with me first, and, despite his small frame, his stare sets me on edge, as if I should be ready for a fight I can't win. He's small, wire like, and his hands are wrapped, ready to punch someone out. "Autumn Alderidge." His greeting lacks any warmth.

"Louie Alderidge," I respond in a similar tone to the ten-year-old.

"There is my beautiful niece!" Uncle says, a large smile on his face. "How was the travel out here?" Harvey and Sam slip past and nod toward me as they make their way upstairs. They look ready to collapse in bed and enjoy being away from my uncle. Staying in shape is important in this business. Training makes that a reality.

"I was able to sleep through it," I respond with a smile.

Uncle gives a hearty laugh, comes over, and sits on the other end of the couch. "I always say if you can sleep on a helicopter, you're either drugged, dying, or have an amazing pilot. Who was your pilot? A Wright, I assume?"

The Wrights are a minor family, descending from an illegitimate child of one of the Wright brothers who created the first plane. They pride themselves on having a monopoly on aircrafts.

"Rule seven," Ashlynn reminds, and Uncle bats a hand through the air at his daughter as if to cast her words away. *Assume Nothing.*

"The rules exist for a reason." The way she says it, her tone light and playful, I bet my uncle has told her that many times.

"Go to bed, Ashlynn," Uncle orders.

Ashlynn gives me one last steely look before she picks up her knives and departs, leaving me alone in the living room with my uncle. Perhaps Ashlynn is so harsh to me because her father dismisses her like she's nothing. I may feel like I'm treated like a child, and not let in on anything, but my father would never talk to me like that. Uncle has tried to protect her, but all he's done is given her too normal of a life to fit in here, and too much of here to fit into the normal world.

"I believe it was a Wright," I say once Ashlynn has left.

Everything here is a domino line of secrets and I'm trying to tip one in the middle.

Uncle nods. "The folder, Autumn."

Right. I slide the folder out from where I sit on it and pass it to my uncle. "I haven't looked at it yet," I say as Uncle begins to riffle through the pages inside. "Is it related at all to my mission?"

My uncle slowly nods his head, but his words contradict him. "No. Not yet at least. We need to know the level of security that house has. Most around here have the standard stuff—if they have security at all. Many lake cabins are left unlocked."

"But what about the fifth family?"

"They were abolished over sixty years ago."

"But—"

Uncle snaps the folder shut, a stern expression on his face. My father makes the same one when he wants everyone to be quiet. "Just because you're third in line for the throne, doesn't mean you are entitled to know everything that is happening, understood?"

"Understood."

"Your father has you on a need-to-know protective-bubble policy. Trust me, Autumn, you don't need to worry about this. What you should be worried about is finding Kato and getting close." Uncle pulls a different folder seemingly from thin air and hands it to me. "This is your mission. It's Kato's file from your Aunt Magdalena. Study it. You start tomorrow."

My hand runs over the manilla file Uncle has handed me. When I open it, he leaves me alone.

Kato. A terrible name. A soap opera name. I repeat it mockingly in my head.

His mother passed away when he was young, leaving him to be raised by his father and their butler. Most of the information in his profile is dry. Basic and unexciting. Kato is a model student at Phelps High, home of the fighting knights, with great grades and a football scholarship to Notre Dame, contingent on how he plays his senior season. He's well-rounded, too, helping with school musicals and singing in the school choir. He's a member of the National Honor Society and goes hunting with his father. He won a couple school spelling bees when he was younger and loves escape rooms. There are a few other likes and dislikes, including that he has a fondness for blondes, a feature I have that my cousin does not, probably why I was chosen instead of her.

Reaching the end of the folder, I flip through it again.

I don't find a photo of him.

Aunt Magdalena always includes a photo if one exists. How could a star football player and a member of the show choir not have a photo in his folder? Come to think of it, most escape rooms also take your picture, another source Aunt Magdalena could have accessed. I scan through the folder one last time. Without a photo, I'll be flying blind.

"Well, this will be fun."

RULE 5:

YOU ARE YOUR MOST POWERFUL
WEAPON.

The next morning, I lay the folder and its contents out on my bed. Kato's favorite color is green, which makes sense for a Northland boy who spends free time in the woods hunting.

I pull on a green sweater Marleen left me in the closet. I smooth it out over my jeggings and a tight pink top my mother must have packed for me. When I'm not in mission gear, I like vintage suits, large, oversized sweaters, baggy Ts, and baggy jeans. I wish that I had packed my duffel. If I had, it wouldn't be full of clothes that look like someone is trying to give me a Princess-Diary-style makeover. I have clothes here in my room on the island, but most of them are tight after two years of absence from the Northwoods. And my duffel is packed with clothes that are tight for a very different reason.

I can't bring myself to care too much. The faster I catch his eye and finish the mission, the sooner I can justify going to London, meeting up with the rest of my family, and figuring out what is going on. Whether they are okay or not, I try to push the worrying thought from my mind.

A soft knock raps my door, and I open it, hoping it's

Marleen. My face falls at the sight of Ashlynn standing there instead. "Hi."

"You don't need to look so disappointed, Princess." Ashlynn leans against the door jamb, her eyes going to the open folder on the bed. She nods at it. "Everything on Kato?"

"Except a photo," I comment and move back to the bed to gather up the pages and close the folder, blocking the information from her view.

"Play nice, Princess. You know, I know Kato."

"Is that why you weren't picked for the mission? You've already scared him away with your fangs?" I cross my arms and stare down my cousin. "What do you want, Ashlynn?"

"I could help maybe. Give you some pointers." The look on Ashlynn's face tells me her offer isn't out of kindness.

I want to accept, but my pride isn't going to let me. "I've got this, Ashlynn." I try to sound confident even though I most certainly do not have this. The thought of romancing anyone makes my stomach churn.

I was told at age eight that I would marry Dimitri of the Daxterov family. Knowing I was already engaged zapped my desire to date, and I only ever saw family and members of other families—they saw me as an opportunity, not a person—at the manor. I played with knives, created poisons, and planned my fight moves. Though I tend to often fail at combat, I still prefer spending my free time with that than romance.

I want my family to be safe and to hide in Paris with Aunt Magdalena until the Daxterovs force me to come to Russia.

This is going to be the summer from Hell. I can already tell.

"You don't have anything, Princess. Kato isn't going to know your status, so he isn't going to trip over himself to get a look at you, like the boys from other families you usually meet."

No boy has ever tripped over himself to look at me, but I don't correct her. "Yeah, Ashlynn, I know."

"When was the last time you seduced someone on a mission?"

Never. My first real mission without my parents had been two days ago, and I had run in and run out without getting caught, thanks to Quinton's quick thinking. This is my first solo mission, which is a big deal in my family.

Ashlynn gives a small laugh at my silence. "Yeah, that's what I thought. You're going to fail this."

"I'm not going to fail, Ashlynn," I mutter, looking back at my folder, my face burning red.

She is right. She has been trained for this. But I'm trained, too. And I will lead a family one day. How can I do that if I couldn't even stand my ground against my own cousin?

I stand a little taller, fire in my eyes as I meet her gaze. "Maybe if you spent more time training and less time on makeup, you'd know that, and you'd know I am more than qualified for this mission. It's my brother who will take over your trust fund one day, and I will be heading the Daxterovs with my husband, meaning I will hold influence over two of the four major families. So, I suggest you stop treating me like a screwup when I'm more qualified than you." The words pour from my mouth before I even fully process them.

I move to shove past Ashlynn—she's a good inch taller in her five-inch heels—stopping so we're wedged under the door frame, and say, "Sleep with one eye open, 'Princess,' because the queen just arrived, and you've pissed her off."

AUTUMN

AGE 16

"**F**ailure is not an option. If you fail in the field, you are dead," my mother offered the reminder through the headset I wore.

My fingers were freezing as I stared helplessly at the wires in front of me.

"Fix the gate, Autumn; it will be good practice," I mocked under my breath, echoing my father's words. He was trying to get me out of the house and had run out of other tasks for me to do. Part of me suspected he had smashed the gate lock himself. Though nothing looked smashed.

I jammed the butt of my mini flashlight into my mouth and crouched down, sticking my hand into the box to examine the wires. Similar enough to bomb wiring but different enough to leave me confused.

"You're sixteen, Autumn. You can fix a gate," my mother offered more assurance into my ear. "I'm going off headset now. I'll see you once the gate is fixed."

I shook my head and continued to examine the wires in the frigid winter night air. How did age make you eligible to fix gate wiring?

I turned at the low hum of an engine. A car made its way from the house down to the gate. I put my hand up to block the glare of the headlights as I moved to open the gate manually.

"Don't bother!" a voice called as the headlights on the car went

43

dark, and a boy about my age emerged from the backseat, a long coat wrapped around himself.

I blinked a few times until my eyes readjusted to the darkness, and I removed the flashlight from my mouth to point it at the young man. I didn't recognize him. He must be the guest my father had been doing everything in his power to keep me from meeting.

"Evening," I greeted with a nod. "The gate is out; I can just open it manually for you."

"Pretty girl like you? No. Come on, ve vill fix the gate together," he said with a thick Russian accent.

"What's your name?" I called as the wind pulled my hair back from my face and turned my cheeks a rosy red.

The boy stepped forward, removing his bomber hat and revealing a mess of brown hair. He smiled as he came over and placed his hat on my head. "You're going to freeze your ears off vithout a hat on."

"My knight in shining armor," I said before sticking the flashlight back in my mouth and straightening the hat on my head.

"I am Dimitri Daxterov."

I nearly dropped the flashlight from my mouth. "Dimitri?" I mumbled. I removed it from my mouth and stuffed it in my pocket. Still turned on, the flashlight made the front of my pants glow.

Dimitri Daxterov.

The boy my parents had arranged for me to marry.

Dimitri gave a laugh. "You know, I alvays thought our first time meeting vould be far more romantic, Autumn Alderidge."

I smiled. "Of course, you know who I am."

"The painting of your family in the entryvay gives you avay as the prettiest girl I vill ever meet."

I rolled my eyes. "Okay, smooth-talking Russian, but can you fix a gate box?"

Dimitri ran a gloved hand through his thick brown hair, his smile unwavering. "Let's take a look." He went over to the box, crouching down in front of it. "Ah, yes. I know vhat's vrong."

"Really?" I asked in surprise. I leaned down—everything had

looked fine to me. Perhaps the Daxterovs also specialized in gate fixing. Another reason I wasn't going to fit in.

"It's alveady fixed." He turned his head up as he spoke, our faces a lot closer than I expected.

"It's already fixed?" I echoed and took an awkward step back.

He stood. "Your mother vanted us to meet, but your father, he's a stern man and serious about keeping you hidden. I thought when I came to America I vould get a fairy tale first look at my future vife, but alas, this is so much better. Already I know so much about you."

"Well now, that's not a creepy thing to say at all." My mother had suggested to my father that I be the one to investigate the gate.

Dimitri reached past me, so close I could detect his body heat and the smell of both his cologne and the smoke left by a bonfire. He hit the "OPEN" button, and sure enough, the gate swung open. "I vill send one of my family's men to come here to America and serve as your gate man. My future vife should not have to bother herself vith matters such as gates."

Before I could speak, Dimitri reached down and gently grabbed my hand, kissing it through my glove in the dark as if I were a lady, and he a gentleman, instead of us being teens standing in the freezing cold.

"Until ve meet again, my love."

RULE 6:

HIT THE ELEVATOR BUTTON AND TAKE
THE STAIRS.

According to Aunt Magdalena's folder, Kato likes ice cream and inline skating, neither of which strikes me as odd or helpful. What would be helpful is a picture so I could approach him if I see him. I can't walk all over town and stop every guy who looks about my age and ask if he is Kato, especially since I'm not supposed to know him yet.

Part of me regrets not taking Ashlynn up on her offer to help as I tie the pontoon, the same one Marleen had used to run into town, to a public dock in the tiny town of Phelps at the eastern end of the lake. On shore, a walkway through a well-kept garden of bright flowers sneaks up a small hill to a dirt lot. In the distance, a little red and yellow ice cream parlor I remember visiting the last time I was here comes into view.

Ashlynn could have at least given me an idea where to find him. Instead, my plan is to roam the nearby small towns and pray I somehow overhear or see something that tips me off as to who this guy is. I have all summer, after all, even if I want this to be over as soon as possible.

Once I am confident the boat is secure, I tuck the pontoon key in my pocket, push my hair out of my face, and stand to turn. I turn too fast, though, and nearly run headfirst into

47

someone. With a yelp, I spring back. My foot slips on a piece of seaweed on the dock, my feet fly out, and I'm left desperately grabbing at the air. But there's nothing to grab, and I plunge into the cold, murky water.

I try to close my mouth, but the disgusting lake water fills it. I hit the sandy bottom, my hair exploding into a yellow halo around my head, like a fallen angel. I try to get my feet under me, but in the water it's hard to move. My hand tangles in a weed similar to the culprit of my fall and I pull, trying to break free. I end up tearing the weed out by its roots, causing a cloud of dirt to billow around my face, making it even harder to see.

I close my eyes, spinning myself upright, my foot hitting the bottom. There's a splash next to me. Then something grabs me around the waist, and I am being pulled toward the surface.

I break through the water and am pushed up onto the dock. I give a cough, emptying my mouth of the disgusting lake water. A woman in a white apron stands clapping outside the ice cream parlor. A mother and a young boy on the sidewalk also clap—as well as a group of high schoolers in the garden, one leaning on a "No Weapons Allowed" sign. I scan the faces. So many kids my age. I pull my sopping wet hair from my face and hope one of the boys is wearing something monogrammed with a 'K,' but no luck.

My rescuer offers his hand. I take it and stand up, recognizing him as the boy I dodged on the dock before falling into the lake.

"Sorry," I mutter, noticing he is also dripping wet, his Plum Ski-ters Water Ski Show T-shirt clinging to his chest. He, too, pushes hair out of his face. He doesn't look upset, though. In fact, he holds a humored smile on his lips and waves at the people clapping.

I instantly hate him.

How pompous. I would have been fine. I could have gotten myself out.

"Don't be sorry," he says, looking down at me with piercing blue eyes, the smile staying on his lips. "Sorry I startled you. I was coming to see if you needed a hand tying off the boat."

I cross my arms in front of my dripping wet form. "Because you don't think I can tie a boat? Why, because I'm a girl?"

His smile falters for a moment. "No, beautiful, it's because you're a tourist. Welcome to Phelps. Most tourists can't tie a boat or hook a nightcrawler. Some drive boats and stand on the edge of docks and can't even swim."

"Oh ha, ha. I can swim. I was just enjoying the company of the perch down there, until you decided to play hero for the crowd." That sounds stupid, even for me, but I press on with it anyway. "I don't need your help, and I'm not a tourist."

"Okay, beautiful."

"Don't call me that."

He gives a small laugh, pushing his wet hair back again, though it is no use. "Would you rather I call you ugly?"

"I'd rather you call me Autumn." Shoot. *Rule three: never use your real name on a mission.* I don't even know this guy, and I'm already breaking rules. With any luck he'll vanish into the backdrop of my life.

"Okay. 'Autumn.' And you're not a tourist. But I've never met you before. Are you new to the area?"

"Something like that." I glance at the group of teenagers. They've dispersed and are headed toward the ice cream shop. If it operates like a Starbucks, they might announce the kids' names when their orders are ready. "I have to go," I say with a smile, trying to paint on civility so he'll step out of my way. I could shove him into the lake instead, but I'd rather not make him an enemy, no matter how arrogant he seems. If he knows Kato, I may be able to use him to get to my target.

He extends his still wet hand for a handshake before letting me pass. "I'm Kato, by the way."

Kato?

Oh, crap.

"Kato. Nice name."

It really isn't. I have never met a decent person named Kato—or anyone named Kato—nor has there ever been a decent Kato in, well, anything I have ever read or watched.

I take his wet hand in mine and shake it.

This is my target, and I've told him my real name and been incredibly rude to him.

"You have a good handshake," he comments, still wearing that cocky smile.

Can I punch him? How am I supposed to respond to that? Compliment his handshake back? "Can I buy you an ice cream as a thank you for pulling me out of the lake?" I offer, trying to steer this back into focus.

Kato's smile grows. "I would love that, Autumn." He uses my name as if it feels good for him to rub it in that I broke a rule. Not that he would know.

We curve up the stairs through the garden, across the dirt lot to the shop that looks more picturesque from afar. Closer up, the building's yellow paint is starting to chip, and its faded red trim is full of cobwebs with mosquito carcasses trapped in them. Two-hour parking signs line the road, and small green banners with the photos of high schoolers and the letters PHS for Phelps High School hang from light posts. Each photo bears a senior's name, a public celebration of their graduation. As I pass, I try to act like a normal teen and study a few—Zoey, Charity, Xiao, Sam, Cody, Brooke.

Kato opens the door for me into Sweets, Treats and More. Inside, rows of ice cream buckets sit encased behind a curved window. A small aisle full of candy runs to the right, and down a couple stairs to the left is a cozy sitting area, where the group of teens is settled, paying us no mind.

An older woman with short curly brown hair stands behind the counter. I wonder if one of the high school seniors is hers. Her dusty-blue apron stretches as crisp across her plump frame, as her smile does on her face.

"What kind do you like?" Kato asks.

Even though he stands behind me as I consider the flavors, I feel him watching me.

I have never been given so many ice cream choices before. Whenever Quinton and I got ice cream, which isn't often, as my mother is lactose intolerant, it is bought for us and typically plain old vanilla. On occasion we would get caramel swirl.

"I don't know," I admit and turn to look back at the dripping-wet, curly-haired boy with a pleasant smile. He has kind eyes; his Adam's apple does a slow bob as he studies me in return. Perhaps he truly had been trying to help earlier. Afterall, there's no way he could have known who I am. He saw someone in need of help, and rather than standing by, he came to my rescue. It was kind of heroic and it helped that he looked like a hero.

Stop. What the hell was I thinking? My mouth sours, and I make sure those terrifying thoughts truly were internal. He doesn't appear any smugger, so I must be good. I clear my throat and force my mind back to the problems at hand. "What would you recommend, Kato?"

"My favorite is blue moon."

"Blue moon? Isn't that a type of beer?" Beer-flavored ice cream sounds terrible, though it would be my luck that the first time I get to pick my own ice cream I get stuck ordering beer-flavored as part of a mission.

Kato looks at me like I just slapped him across the face, a look I know rather well. I've been trained on the best, most effective ways to slap people. During training, when people know it's coming, they still make that same face—the one Kato wears right now.

"No," he answers in horror. "Blue moon is the best kind of ice cream ever. It is not beer."

"It's also a brand of beer," the woman behind the counter offers, her voice holding the maternal warmth I would associate with a small-town mom. "What can I getcha?"

Before I can say anything else, Kato orders two double-scoop bowls of blue moon.

He has ordered for me without consulting me. I might never get to choose what ice cream I want again, and even here, when I thought I would have a choice, he now has taken it from me. That little flicker of anger I have for him that had started to fade, sparks up in my chest.

This mission is going to be terrible. If I could beat him up or kidnap him or force feed him a vial of poison that would knock the smug smile off his face and leave him writhing on the floor, it would be a far more pleasant and easy mission. If Ashlynn was trained in seduction, lesson one must be how to not punch your target in the face when you really want to. I am not well-trained for this.

Kato hands me my bowl and uses a credit card to pay the lady.

The ice cream is blue and appears to have no chunks. I take a bite, and oh my gosh, it's as if fruit and cotton candy had a baby in my mouth.

I must admit, it's good, even if I don't like someone else ordering for me. Or paying for both of us when I offered to buy him ice cream.

"Good, right?" Kato asks with an eager smile as he holds the door open again so we can take our treats outside.

I shrug, stepping back onto the cracked sidewalk. "It's pretty good. But I said I would pay."

"Don't worry about it. You can get it next time."

Next time?

I smile at Kato. "Sounds good. I hope to see you around, Kato. Thank you."

"You're not going to eat that with me?" he asks with a hint of a frown.

For my mission, I probably should. But right now, I'm not

sure if I can keep myself from saying something harsh I'll regret later. I'm dripping wet, angry, and miserable. It would be better to count my losses from today and try again soon. Hit when I'm back to being my fresh criminal self.

"Well, Autumn, if you're not too busy falling off docks later on, there's a group of us going to the roller rink in town. You should meet us there. Five o'clock?"

I nod my head. "Sounds like fun."

"I'll see you later then."

"We'll see." That's what I say, but I know I have to be there. I have to kiss up to this jerk, who thinks I'm helpless, until he takes me to his house. I anticipate that should be easy, seeing the type of guy he is.

"Okay." Kato nods and turns, heading toward the shore.

I watch him go. The pompous, arrogant, jerk of a teenage boy who doesn't even let me pick my own ice cream. And now I need to spend my summer getting as close to him as possible. How did I get this unlucky?

AUTUMN

AGE 16

I held the pack of ice Abby had handed me against my lip. Despite my best efforts, I could already feel it swelling. Abby drove the helicopter and flew us away, back toward home.

"I hate my birthday," I said to her through the headset.

"Ya hate them cause ya parents keep tryin' to murder ya. I don't get this trainin' ya and Quinton have to do."

I smiled at Abby. "I'm lucky to have a friend like you. I'm glad you joined our family, though probably not as glad as Quinton is." I held my smile as I looked at Abby, but it quickly faded when she furrowed her brow and switched on autopilot.

Abby turned to me. "What's that supposed to mean?" she demanded, her usual humor gone.

My face fell and my blood turned warm. "I just meant—I'm sorry. I didn't mean anything."

"Yar a terrible liar for a spy, girlie."

"I'm not a spy," I argued as I looked down at my other hand. A slash marred the back of it from my cousin Opal's whip. Birthday trainings didn't count as real missions, as my family would never kill me. But they sure hurt like the real deal.

"Does Quinton like me?"

"Abby!" I shook my head at my loss for words. What could I say

55

that wouldn't get me into any more trouble with her? I thought she knew that I knew. But maybe I was wrong. Maybe my deduction was off. And if I was, and she told my parents, that would open another can of trouble.

A smile spread on Abby's lips, and she busted out laughing. "He better like me. We've been dating for a few months now. How long have ya known?"

My mouth fell agape. "I didn't know."

"Well, now ya do."

I looked at my lap again. How could I not have known that my brother and Abby were dating? When Abby came to the manor when I was eleven, Quinton and I would mimic her accent, pretending we were from Scotland, too. Abby had straight up decked Quinton when he had put on my plaid skirt, called it a kilt, and mocked the way Abby talked. I had sensed something change between the two of them, ever since our last trip to Gangster Island. But I hadn't known they were dating. I felt like a terrible sister and an even worse Alderidge.

"Don't feel bad. Quinton wanted it kept a secret from ya parents, and yar not good at keepin' secrets," Abby assured, as if that should make me feel better. "What if me and you had a secret, too?"

"Like what?" A smile formed at the corners of my mouth.

"Well, if I have to come and keep savin' ya, what if we had a code, to, ya know, let each other know things are okay? A secret code, one not even Quinton is in on."

"Okay. What if...if everything is fine, I ask you your favorite color, and you say yellow?"

"Yellow. I like it."

"If things are bad, say purple, okay?"

"Okay. And blue if it's about yar brother."

RULE 7:

ASSUME NOTHING.

M arleen squeals with joy when I tell her I'm going to a roller rink. She says nothing about me being wet. My first reaction to someone returning to my house smelling of lake water and saying in an agitated voice that they have to go roller skating would be very different.

After I shower the lake off me, I find retro '80s clothes on my bed and Marleen sitting eagerly in the corner of my room. I am grateful for her help, but something feels wrong about everything she laid out.

I put my damp hair up in a denim scrunchy and choose a leather vest and gray *Breakfast Club* graphic T-shirt, the only shirt that isn't neon, or has a hideous pattern.

"I recommend the leather skirt," Marleen says with a grin. "Oh! Or the leopard print skirt. You are going to want a skirt."

"I think I'll just stick with my leggings." These skirts are a lot shorter than what I'm used to.

"If you want to '80s dress to impress, you should pick one of the skirts," Marleen presses. What is with everyone wanting me to dress differently? First the duffel, now Marleen. I know this is a mission, and I should suck it up and take her advice, but mission or not, it's also the first time a boy my age has ever asked me to go anywhere. Kato is the closest thing I have ever had to a date.

"I need to dress in something that won't distract me from my mission," I say.

And much to Marleen's displeasure, I stick with my modern dark leggings.

As I leave, Ashlynn stops me in the hall. "You already have a date, don't you?" she asks with a shake of her head.

"I do." I try to sidestep her, but she steps with me.

"Watch out for Vy."

"Who's Vy?"

"Viona. She's possessive of Kato. I could help, you know, keep her away. Be a part of the mission. It would be no trouble. If you need help. I have '80s clothes, too. Or I'm sure Marleen would be happy to play dress up on me as well."

I try to sidestep Ashlynn again, and again she moves with me. "No. Thank you." As much as her help would be useful, albeit annoying, I have to turn her down.

I don't know why she's being so helpful. Maybe she's trying to steal my mission from me. Or maybe pretending to be Mary from Phelps is so boring she would even help me for an excuse to leave the house.

Mary is her identity when she's outside of the island. She gets a life away from murder and training and missions. She goes to school and proms and pep rallies. Though I struggle to imagine Ashlynn being peppy.

Whatever her intention is, I wish she would just stay out of my way. If she comes with me, she will learn that I broke a rule and am breaking another by not reporting it to my uncle. You don't break rules in our family, and she no doubt would take great joy in telling everyone.

"Don't say I didn't warn you," Ashlynn says in her usual tone, before finally moving out of the way.

If she is trying to get in my head, it is working. By the time I reach Twin Skates—a faded blue one-story square of bricks in the center of a weedy parking lot, with an even more faded roller skate painted over the door—I am all nerves. I had been nothing but rude to Kato earlier, and whoever this Vy is might mess up the connection I need to make with Kato to infiltrate his house. Failing my first solo mission is not an option.

So, I put on a brave face and enter the darkness.

Neon and black lights glow from the walls. A disco ball over the oval-shaped rink sends white dots dancing everywhere. The screechy sounds of the "Get'cha Head in the Game" from the *High School Musical* soundtrack pierces my ears. The scar on my forearm is obvious in this lighting, making me wish I had long sleeves on. I wrap my arms around myself and look for Kato but keep an eye out for this Vy character.

I spot Kato out on the rink, laughing with a few other teenage boys. The others look softer edged than Kato. Their outfits are more wrinkled and thrown together, where it looks like Kato took time to pick his clothes out. The others look more relaxed, like they could fade away until the only person left on the rink is Kato with his piercing eyes. He's not the only one out there though. I recognize one of them, Cody, from one of the high school senior banners in Phelps.

My eyes lock with Kato's across the room, and I offer a wide smile. Hoping I'm coming off as confident, I wave.

"You came!" he exclaims over Troy Bolton's crooning about his conflicted feelings. Kato rushes toward me and rolls into the half-wall separating the rink from the carpeted area where I stand. The bright, lopsided grin on his face makes me smile back a little bigger before I can catch myself. What is wrong with me?

"You invited me," I say. Unsure if he can hear me over the music, I add a shrug. His enthusiasm to see me is beyond what I expected. It seems, I don't know, off. But also, sweet.

Kato straightens up. "Wait, let me come to you," he yells, inching along the wall to an opening in it a few feet away. He steps through and walks his skates over. Before he reaches me, though, one of his skates slips forward on a smooth patch of carpet, and he rolls into me. I'm quick to react and steady him before our meeting turns into a collision.

"Sorry!" he exclaims. His body is so close, his breath feathers my forehead. "I guess we're both a little clumsy today."

I take a step back, my lips pursed together. If he comes roller skating often enough that Aunt Magdalena put it in her file, I suspect he should be skilled enough not to slip into me. Maybe he's nervous because he likes me. A smile comes to my lips, but I bat it away. "It's good to see you."

"Yeah, it's good to see you, too. Have you gotten your skates yet?"

"Not yet. I just got here."

"M'lady." He holds out his arm for me to take.

Confused, but without arguing, I take it. I need to gain some connection with this boy before the girl Ashlynn warned me about shows up. But part of me wonders if my mission is worth being nice to him when more skilled operatives are at my family's fingertips. My arm takes his, and he leads me over to the counter where a girl has her back to us.

"A pair of skates, please." Kato smiles at me. "What size shoe are you, beautiful?"

"I said don't call me beautiful." The words slip out before I can stop them. *Nice going, Autumn.* I cover it with a smile. "I'm a size nine."

"Ugly will take a size nine," Kato says with a grin directed at me.

"That's not a nice way to be blatherin' about her, laddie." The girl behind the counter has a familiar thick Scottish accent.

I nearly choke on my own spit as Abby turns around, tugging on the edge of her oversized Twin Skates shirt, which hangs on her body despite her curves. A lopsided name tag,

"Jenny," dangles below the collar. Abby places the skates down on the counter with a thud that pulls me back to reality.

"Are you okay?" Kato asks, a worried look on his face. "It looked like you zoned out there for a moment."

"I'm fine." I push a smile back on my lips. Had my parents asked Abby to come and watch over me? Or did she come with a message that couldn't wait until I was home tonight? My mind flashes to my brother as Kato lifts the skates off the counter and offers me his arm again.

"What's your favorite color?" I ask Abby, even though I sense Kato's eyes watching me. I don't care if I'm confusing him. I would throw the whole mission and leave now if Quinton was in trouble. Ashlynn could come and deal with Kato as well as I can.

Please don't say blue.

Abby smiles at me. "Favorite color? What an odd thing. I would say pink."

"Pink?" Pink isn't one of the colors from our code. Has she forgotten? She got to date my brother, and I got a code she couldn't even remember?

"The poofy color," Abby says, as if that clarifies.

I nod my head and turn. My mind is a buzz of disbelief and concern for my brother.

"Not the color you wanted her to say?" Kato asks, catching me off guard.

"What's your favorite color?" I step a little closer as he moves toward the benches for taking on and off skates. I smell the faint fragrance of lake water and bonfire smoke on him. The scent of the pristine outdoors of northern Wisconsin.

Kato puts an arm around me, and I try to relax my shoulders so they're not tense under his touch. "I would say my favorite color is green."

"Green?" I try to sound interested, but I already know his favorite color is green from my file.

"Is that how you respond whenever someone tells you their

favorite color? Repeat it as a question?" he asks with a laugh, and we stop at the benches.

I think that's a joke, but I'm only half listening to him right now. Every possible reason Abby might be here clouds my mind, and of course my brain isn't creating any positive ones. I move out from under his arm and sit down, sliding off my sneakers and taking the skates from him with a wordless thanks. It could be nothing. Abby could just be my backup. But it doesn't feel like nothing.

"Sorry, I meant that as a joke. I'm not great at... Forget I said that," he says softly.

I look up from tying my skates. Embarrassment colors his face. "I'm not upset, not at all! I was just—" And then rule nine comes to me all of a sudden: *all information can be used against you.* "My mind just feels a little elsewhere tonight. I think it might be the loud music."

"Sensory overload?" he speculates. "My grandma, she gets that so bad, we haven't been able to come visit in years. Being in the car or an airport or any small, enclosed space can trigger her. Also, if more than one person is talking at once or if there are a lot of noises. But we all tend to get it from time to time."

"Kato!" A boy in a muscle T-shirt skates over and punches Kato in the arm. "You coming back out on the floor or what?"

"Seb," Kato greets, stringing an arm around his friend and spinning him on his skates to face me. "Meet Autumn."

I wish he would stop pointing out that he knows my name, but he's not doing anything out of the ordinary.

"Hi." I stand, one foot in a skate and the other with only a sock on, trying to hold my balance. I put out a hand for Seb to shake.

"I'm a hugger," Seb says. He moves away from Kato and pulls me into a bro hug, patting me so hard on the back I feel like I'm getting the Heimlich. Seb pulls away and holds me at arm's length.

He looks familiar.

"I saw you earlier today. Kato shoved you in the water so he could look like a hero in front of everyone."

That must be how I recognize him. He was a part of the group on the shore. I look around the rink and spot every member of that group here. Are they all Kato's friends? I don't want to meet them all.

"I did not shove her!" Kato exclaims. Seb laughs, which makes me smile. At least Kato's friends have a good sense of humor.

"Don't let him hog you all the time, okay, Autumn? I'll see you later, Kato," Seb says before skating away.

"He seems nice." I sit back down and slide on my other skate.

Kato nods in my peripheral vision. "Yeah, Seb is great. If you're here this fall, you'll get to know everyone a lot better."

"I won't be here..." I trail off, wanting to assure both myself and him that I will be long gone when the leaves start turning colors—but that all depends on Kato. If he lets me in his house tonight after a fun night of skating, I might be able to talk my way into being in London by the weekend. Then again, maybe Abby showed up to pull me from the mission altogether, and we can leave tonight, Kato's house be damned. I look up at Kato after tying my skate, and he stares at me, waiting for me to finish my sentence. "I'm home-schooled," I tack on. It's not a lie. Technically, I suppose, I am.

Kato nods. "Cool. Then you'll just have to meet everyone sooner than later."

"Right." I glance at the rink, unsure if I can even stand with wheels on my feet. Roller skating has never been part of my training.

"Hey, if you don't want to do this, we could go somewhere else," Kato offers; he must sense my hesitance.

Are my emotions painted that clearly on my face? My mom would be disappointed if she knew I wasn't hiding something as simple as nerves over skating. I hear her in my mind scolding me: *"How do you think you'll be able to keep Kato on the hook if you're so easily read?"*

I smile at Kato, praying if I ask him to leave, he'll see it as an opportunity to take advantage of me. "Maybe we can go somewhere quieter?" I offer.

He pauses for a moment, as if trying to figure out what I mean before he nods. "Yeah, of course." He sits down next to me, sliding his skates off. I follow suit. From where we sit, I can kill him about twenty different ways. The thought calms my nerves against the reality of going somewhere I've never been with someone much larger than me.

"Kato!" A shrill female voice fills my ears over the music. I tense and look up to find a girl bounding over in street shoes. She wears a cherry-red top that matches her glossy lips. Her dark chocolate hair is tied up in a high pony that swishes with each step. *Viona.* Has to be. Without even meeting her, I know this is the girl Ashlynn warned me about. She's tall even without heels, and gorgeous, and clearly likes Kato, based on the look she gives me.

Kato stands in socked feet as Viona comes over and wraps her arms around him in a hug. "Hey, Vy," he greets in a warm tone. This is the type of girl I imagine with someone named Kato, not me. "I didn't think you were coming out tonight. I thought your parents said you weren't allowed."

"Who's your friend?" Viona asks, a chill to her tone. She pulls away from Kato and twirls her hair around her finger. She gently bites at her lip in a seductive way that I'm sure if I did, I would look like I was nibbling at dry, flaky mouth skin.

"Right. Vy, meet Autumn. Autumn is new to town, and I was just going to show her around a little. Autumn, this is my friend Viona."

"Nice to meet you." I don't stand. I turn my attention back to my skates so I can finish untying them.

"You're leaving already?" Vy pouts at Kato. "I thought

maybe we could hang out tonight. At least have one couples' skate."

"Autumn isn't feeling well, so we were just going to head out," Kato explains to Vy, grabbing a pair of tennis shoes from under the bench to slip on. "Another time, Vy. You should probably head home before your parents see you snuck out again."

"Oh, come on, Kato." Vy places a hand on Kato's shoulder, her painted nails a forest-green hue. Kato's favorite color isn't much of a secret, apparently. I cannot wait until I get out of this small town. "She'll be fine for one song."

I glance back at the counter, where Abby sprays disinfectant into the returned skates. She looks so natural and comfortable, despite this not being her job at all. Everyone else in my family excels at blending in. Me, I tend to be a loud klutz who can't hide her feelings. It feels lonely to be an outsider in a world you've spent your whole life trying to fit into. That's the real reason I want to go to Paris. Observation and data analysis and Paris with Aunt Magdalena: that's more me. At least, I hope it is. Because I don't belong here, and it shows.

Abby catches my eye and then her gaze falls on Vy and Kato talking. She grabs the loudspeaker microphone and taps it twice before interrupting the music, "All right skaters, sorry to interrupt ya, but we have a missin' ID card belongin' to someone named Viona. 'Parently, someone isn't as graceful as she appears. Would Viona please come to the counter and retrieve yar ID card?"

"I think that's you," I say to Viona. She doesn't mirror my sweet smile and instead shoots daggers back in my direction.

"Next time then," Vy says to Kato before turning and heading for where Abby stands behind the counter.

"Sorry about her." Kato finishes tying his shoes. "She's actually really nice once you get to know her. It's just the getting to know her part that's tricky."

"I'm sure," I mutter and finish tying my shoes. When I look up, Kato offers a hand for me to take. "What a gentleman," I say and take his hand to get to my feet.

Kato gives a laugh and, before I can even reach for skates, picks up both pairs, holding them by their tied-together laces. I glance at Abby, willing her to say something to me as to why she is here, as Kato places our skates on the counter. She says nothing, and we walk out into the night, leaving the '80s neon behind us.

"Where are we headed?" I ask. My mind tries to stay mission-focused, but my thoughts swirl with speculation about my family's well-being. If Abby came, is that a sign they don't need her in London? Which means "good news," right? Or is it to watch over me, which would also be better than her coming here to tell me something had happened to the rest of my family. If Quinton is dead, then I'd need to be escorted to safety since I am next in line after my mother. My arranged marriage would be off then, too, as two heads of two different families aren't permitted to marry since it would merge the families' powers. The four families must remain equal. That would mean my parents would find someone else for me to marry, someone with lower status; I'd probably then have to worry about him slicing my throat in my sleep to take my throne.

"Autumn?"

"Hm?" I realize I had stopped walking and, judging by the look on Kato's face, had missed something he said. "Sorry, what?" I put a bubbly smile on my face. It's in stark contrast to his own expression. His smile is gone, his lips now pressed tight together. His eyes turn down, pulling his eyebrows with them, but remain soft under his eyes. He no longer looks sharp-edged. He's watching me. He's studying me the way I should study him for my mission. Except his consideration appears to come from a place of caring, not one of intellectual study.

"Are you okay?"

"Oh, yeah, I'm fine," I lie, pushing the panicked thoughts from my head. The heavy feelings in my gut and throat can't be budged, though. "Where did you say we were headed?"

"Where do you live? Let me drive you home," Kato offers.

I shake my head. The longer this takes, the longer I'm stuck here. "Really, I'm fine, I just zoned out for a minute. We should do something. See the town."

Kato gives a nod, his smile returning. "Okay. If you're sure."

"Yeah, of course. Where to first?"

"Well, beautiful—"

"Don't call me that."

"Well, *Ugly,* I was thinking—" The *Kim Possible* TV show theme song cuts Kato off. "Sorry," he mutters, fishing his phone out of his pocket. "I've been meaning to change—it's my dad. I'll just be a minute." With a tap, he accepts the call and takes a few steps away from me, turning his back. If his mouth had stayed in view, I could have read his lips. I wish I wasn't playing this part of clueless newbie because then I could get closer and listen.

Screw it. It's not that unusual for someone to eavesdrop, right? I take a few steps closer to Kato, and I can make out a few words here and there. None of it makes sense, though. "I know ... gas ... she's ... I'm not ..." and then a long stretch of silence. "We're not doing that ... family ... she's ... okay." Another long stretch of silence. "I'll be home soon."

I take a quick step back and stare down at my feet, praying he won't know I heard anything, although I have no usable intel.

"I'm really sorry. I have to get home. I, uh, forgot to take the trash out this morning, and he's upset with me."

That's not at all what it sounded like. What did he have to hide? Could this all be linked to why my family seemed so panicked?

"Can I drive you home?" he offers again.

I shake my head. "Thanks, but it's a short walk to the dock. You should get home if your dad is really that upset."

"Yeah." Kato nods but doesn't move. His body language indicates he's trying to decide what to do next, even though it seems like he should just leave. Kato nods, and when he speaks again it's with his head turned, as though he's talking to the dirt parking lot beneath our feet. "Goodnight. I hope to see you around."

"Goodnight, Kato."

AUTUMN

AGE 16

"Where did you get this one?" I asked my father as I ran my hand over the handle of a shiny dagger. Its jeweled handle blinked at me from the shelf, reflecting the bits of dim light it could find inside my father's office. I was looking over his shelf of trinkets and distracting him from whatever he was trying to work on. He didn't mind the distraction. I could always hear in his voice when he was smiling, and now was one of those times.

"Your uncle and I got that on a mission when we were in high school. Best part was that I missed a calculus test."

I turned and looked at my father. "You went to regular high school, right?"

"Yes, as part of our cover, we went to a public high school for my junior year, his sophomore year. Our other three years were spent at Melchior Academy. Or, mine were. Your Uncle went to Hillcrest for his senior year. For a few years future Alderidges were... no longer welcomed at Melchior after I graduated. And before you ask, no, you cannot go there. It's not as welcoming as it was when your uncle and I attended."

"What did you do that you weren't welcomed back?" I asked, meeting my father's gaze.

He opened his mouth to answer, but seemed to think better of it as *he changed the subject. "I actually met your mother my senior year."*

My parents married for love. And what do me and Quinton get?

I sighed and spun in circles in the chair. "What are these?" I asked, gesturing to a stack of folders on his desk. Aunt Magdalena's handwriting marked their covers with different female names.

"Ah," Father breathed and leaned closer. I stopped spinning.

He didn't stop me as I plucked the top folder from the pile and opened it. "Amelia Bancroft," I read, inspecting her photo. "She looks like she's Quinton's age."

"She is." Father nodded as I set Amelia aside and picked up the next folder.

"Amaya Azrail. Also, around Quinton's age." I kept going. "Beth Bindery. The same with Marta Savino. Are you planning an arranged marriage for Quinton?" I hoped it wasn't true as I had just learned he was dating Abby.

Father nodded, confirming my fear.

"You can't do that to him," I argued.

"Why not?" Father asked.

I bit my tongue. I couldn't tell him about Abby and Quinton. That was a secret, one I was sure if my mother learned she would have Abby shipped as far away from my brother as possible.

We all knew deep down that one day this would have to happen for Quinton. The Daxterovs did this same thing when Dimitri was a child. The other families must have found it odd that we had waited so long with Quinton.

But I wanted more for him. I wanted him to be able to marry for love like our parents had, not power, even though the cards were laid out long ago.

"Does Quinton know yet?" I asked.

"No, not yet. The files just came in today. Your aunt has found ten women about your brother's age who would be excellent matches. Your mother and I plan to narrow it down to seven or so, and we'll invite the ladies to our house in a year or two so Quinton can meet them and pick his spouse." And what my father leaves out is that as an Alderidge you must choose to join. No one can make you. Though if any of these

women rejected a proposal from my brother, I'm not sure their families would welcome them back with open arms. "That's how our family has done it for generations. It's not as cold as the Daxterovs, where it's like filling out a job application and never getting an interview, just a yes or no." *A yes or no is still given here, but at least here the people being wed are old enough to understand basic addition.*

"Who do you hope he picks?" *I asked.*

Father rummaged through the files for a moment before pulling one out and handing it to me.

"Naomi Thindrel, youngest daughter of the Thindrel family," *I read.* "You like her because she's one of the four major families?"

"If Quinton picks Naomi, and your marriage to Dimitri goes off without a hitch, the Alderidge family will hold an influence over three of the four major families. Your mother and I would leave behind a stronger legacy and ensure your kids' safety."

I opened another folder belonging to a Karen White, the only girl who didn't have a surname I recognized. She wasn't from a major or minor family. "Why does Quinton get to pick?" *I asked after staring at Karen's file. Based on what Aunt Magdalena found, the possible candidate was a troublemaker with good instincts: No way would she gain my parents' approval and be invited to come to our home. Even if she did, she wasn't part of our world. She wouldn't want to compete. She would never understand.*

"When you didn't, you mean?"

Perhaps Quinton could pick Abby, no matter who our parents invited over. Of course, it would be on him to ask if she could be considered. He didn't even know what was going on.

"Sweetheart, your brother gets to play by our customs and traditions because he's next in line. Since you're not, we couldn't play it how we wanted; we had to play by the Daxterovs' rules. That being said, if Dimitri is not up to your standards, we can always reconsider, and possibly find other arrangements for your future. We just have to be very careful how we go about that, so we don't start a war."

I nodded, opening Sue Koda's file. I was taken aback by the size of her eyes in her photo. "I will do what's best for the family," *I promised.*

RULE 8:

DON'T LEAVE EVIDENCE BEHIND.

As soon as Kato's glowing red taillights slip below the hill and out of sight, I hurry back toward the roller rink, determined to find Abby.

"You forget something?" Vy's voice greets me with all the warmth of an hour-old mug of hot chocolate. She stands in the entryway. Has she been watching me and Kato? How did I not notice? I should have noticed someone watching me. I'm so glad my mother isn't here to see me constantly messing up. Only an amateur misses a tail. And I'm not supposed to be an amateur.

"Uh, yeah." I steady my heart rate, following everything my mother taught me. I don't want to disappoint my family again. Even if they don't know they're being let down. Vy could tell me she is a time traveler come to assassinate me and, right now, I wouldn't react. I should have prepared better and done this from the start with Kato, but I haven't figured him out yet, unlike Vy. Her eyes bare into my soul, like a hawk's talons into the soft flesh of a belly-up walleye. As I reach for the second set of doors, Vy grabs hold of them, preventing me from reentering. "Excuse me, Vy."

"Kato's mine, newbie."

"I think Kato gets a say in that matter," I say, my voice showing no change in emotion.

"I suggest you run home."

I need an excuse to get back inside, and the first one that comes to my mind tumbles out of my mouth. "I had a twenty-dollar bill in my shoe that must have fallen out when I was changing into skates, because it's not there anymore."

"Twenty-dollar bill?"

"Yes." *Let me in.*

Vy shakes her head. "No way you need twenty bucks that much."

"What?"

"Whatever." Vy removes her hand from the door. "Just know I'm watching you."

As I meet Vy's stare, there's something familiar about her expression, as if I had seen her face before today. But how? Where? I take another moment, watching her, both of us daring the other to make a move.

And then it clicks as the past rushes into my head.

"I'll be watching you right back, Karen White," I promise, remembering where I recognize her from: the photo in the folder of possible suitresses for my brother. They were supposed to be coming this next winter—if we have our house back by then. Thankfully, Karen hasn't made the invite list or else she would have already blown my cover. It's easy to get a girl away from your crush if you tell said crush that said girl is a spy sent to take advantage of him.

The way Vy's face pales, I know I nailed it. My mother would be so proud. Though, am I giving away more about myself by revealing I know exactly who she is?

"I suggest you get out of my way, Karen," I say, and Vy takes a step away from the door.

I hurry into the roller rink and go to the counter, but Abby is nowhere to be seen. I curse under my breath and head into the dark night, grateful that Karen is no longer in the entryway, tightening my vest around me as I make my way down to the docks. If Abby was an actual employee I could ask around if people have seen her, but without knowing what her cover is, I don't want to risk exposing her.

Hopefully, Abby is headed back to Gangster Island, and I can talk to her there. I need to know why she is here. I need to know what is going on with my brother and my parents. And I need to know everyone is okay.

A hand grabs my arm. My head snaps to the side. I grab the person and twist their arm with one hand while the other balls into a fist, at the ready. I wriggle myself free and jump into a boxer's stance: fists up guarding my face, feet spread shoulder width.

"Lookie there, yar gettin' better."

Abby's voice relaxes me. I lower my hands. "Abby, what's going on, what are you doing here?" I whisper in case anyone is listening.

Abby looks back toward the roller rink. "Yar parents gave ya the hardest job. Ya really thought they'd send ya alone?"

"Hardest job?" I laugh. "Abby, this is the easiest job of all. I'm scoping out some rich people's house for a monetary gain that probably isn't worth this much work."

Abby shakes her head. "What did yar uncle tell ya?"

"Nothing. Is Quinton okay? You know pink isn't a part of the code," I scold.

Abby smiles. "Ah, that's why I answered 'poofy color.' I saw them yesterday mornin' when they got to the Daxterov property. Autumn, ya need to be smart. The fifth folk is comin' back for revenge. The daughter of the head of the Alderidge folk is prime pickin' and bad news for Kato's father."

"Abby, what are you talking about? They said London, not... not Daxterovs. Not Russia. Is Kato's father tied to all this? Is that why my mission is to get close to Kato to gain intel on the security of his house?"

"Kato's father is the son of the escaped daughter of the

fifth folk. That's how come yar house was abandoned. Kato's father is out for blood. Ya have to get Kato to trust ya and then get in the property. Understand?"

I nod, my mind racing, cold seeping into my body despite the warm air. My hands tremble. "Kato," I say. "Is he in on all of this? Does he know?" I have messed up every step of the way. I fell off the dock, I insulted my target, I've shown my emotions, I revealed my real name, I'm nothing but a prime example of what not to do. And I am the closest one to the biggest threat my family has ever faced. This cannot fall to me. I am not skilled enough for this mission. I was barely skilled enough for it when I thought it was a robbery.

Abby shakes her head. "We don't think so. By the looks of it, his father has tried to shield him from this. He knows nothin'."

"Abby, what if he knows?" Maybe that's why he didn't care when I insulted him. Maybe that's the only reason he seemed to like me. No other guy has ever liked me. It would make sense if it were all fake.

I need to stop worrying about whether he likes me. That is not the concern right now.

"I need to be pulled out. I haven't done any solo work before." It's dangerous. Abby, out of anyone, should see the danger and want to help me. "If they know who I am, if I go in the guy's house, no matter if Kato trusts me or not, I am dead if he sees me. I can't do this; I should be with my family."

Abby shakes her head. "Ya've been training for this yar entire life. Ya got this, okay? Ya gotta be brave. He's not dangerous. He's a high school laddie. Ya've taken down trained assassins in practices. Be brave. And if ya start to feel like ya goin' under, ya uncle and his folk are here with ya. I'll see ya soon, okay?"

I nod, still unsure, but I know it won't help anything to argue with Abby—or back out of the mission I have been given. "Okay. Tell Quinton that Karen White is here."

RULE 9:

ALL INFORMATION CAN BE USED AGAINST YOU.

All information can be helpful, especially when given to the right mind. My mother often says I have the unique ability to solve a mystery with any two clues, even when there is nothing to solve. Though I never know if her words are encouraging or stifling, I know Gangster Island doesn't have the answers about the fifth family, so the next morning I set out for a place in town that might. If the fifth family ended up here, and Kato is related, they should have left some trace.

The library in Phelps reminds me of a shipping container, only a little larger. The Alderidge estate library has beautiful woodwork and stained glass. This library has none of that. Even though it's 82 degrees outside, it's cold and uninviting inside. Rows of books line the walls, and a computer area is located in the center where an old, creepy-looking guy glares at a screen that faces the wall and away from me. I don't want to see what he's looking at and slip past him toward the large sign hung from the ceiling with hardware-store chains that reads "HISTORY."

I brush my fingers past the standard books on World War One, World War Two, the Revolutionary War, and one on Al

Capone. The book I need is buried between *U.S. History 101* and *The History of Food.*

With a hard yank, I pull loose *The History of Phelps.* I flip through the pages and find photos of Marleen's ancestors, the same photos that hang on the walls at Gangster Island. With no other leads to go on, I take it as a good sign. Perhaps there will be something in here that can inform me about the fifth family. Abby's warning has filled in a lot of holes, but I need to know more, and my uncle isn't about to share. Everyone except Marleen and Abby have shielded me from the truth, and I hate it. If I do end up meeting Kato's dad, it's my life on the line.

"Hey!"

I flinch and spin, moving my feet apart to widen my stance, ready again for a fight. But I soften when I see who it is—*Kato.* "You scared me." I smile and attempt to act how a normal girl should, hoping he didn't notice the attack mode. Or that I now know his father is trying to destroy my whole family without him knowing anything about it.

"Sorry about that," Kato replies with a smile. "I was just trying to say hi."

"I'm easily startled. Read one too many ghost stories." I'm pleased with my lie. It's something normal people say, right?

Kato laughs, and I relax a bit. Maybe I can do field work after all. Because of who his dad is, I need a way into his house, and the best way is to make him think I'm a flirtatious girl who likes him. This shouldn't be difficult since he doesn't seem to know who his father really is.

I need to be pleasant, but that's hard to do when you're looking the enemy in the eye, and the face staring back is responsible for uprooting and changing your entire life. His father must think little of our skills, to let his son wander as he does. We could take Kato and use him as leverage. Kato's father must know one of the major four owns the island.

"What brings you to the library?" I ask.

Kato shrugs. "I just had a feeling I should come to the library. I'm glad I did. That and my dad was very insistent I return a book for him this morning."

My cheeks warm at the implication. Oh, God no, am I *blushing?* What is wrong with me? That had to be the worst line ever, followed by a very concerning bit of news. It could have been a coincidence that Kato's dad sent him here, but in my line of work, you learn rather fast that few coincidences ever occur. I may not know much about boys, but I know I would avoid Kato with everything in me if I had my choice. "You should be more careful, or someone will see you talking to the strange new girl."

Kato laughs again. "I hope they do, and I hope they talk about us."

"Us?" I demand. He uses the word with such casual abandon it makes my stomach rock. There is no "us." There was never an "us," and there never could be an "us." I know it's not a written rule but becoming an "us" with your target can't be a good idea, especially when your engaged to a Russian boy whose family is extremely powerful. I pretend to look at the shelf again, even though I have the book I came for in my hand.

"You know, you look really cute when you're trying to be upset with me." Kato brushes his hair out of his face and grins.

"Oh, really?" My brother liked to profile guys like Kato and become friends with them to exploit and, just for fun, watch them combust.

"I think you like me." Kato takes a step closer, leaning against the bookshelf less than a foot away from me.

"I feel absolutely nothing for you."

"Is that so?" His tone is sheer amusement as if he's getting a kick out of this. "Vy texted and said you were really protective of me and a little mean to her after I left the roller rink."

"What?" I spin to look at him. "That is a bald-faced lie."

Kato gives another laugh. "Lie or not, I don't think you feel 'nothing.'"

"Nothing. Come on, Kato, how many girls have you used that line on?" I walk away, book in hand, but he grabs my wrist. It takes all my willpower not to attack him, to end him. I could pin him to the ground in seconds. We could learn just how much his father has taught him.

"I'm sorry," he whispers, seeing the look on my face. Before I can yell at him for grabbing me, his hand lets go.

I can't keep being so brisk with him if I want to succeed in this mission. "Normally, boys take me out before trying to use lines on me." I choke on my own words as they come up, and the taste of stomach acid taints my mouth. I know full well what will come next.

His expression changes into a full-on smile. "Is that so?"

"It is."

"Well then, perhaps I'll just have to take you out. Do you prefer sniper fire or a date?"

A real smile forms on my face, one I try to tamp down. Truthfully, I prefer to get shot by a sniper. I've been trained on how to deal with snipers. No one ever trained me on how to go on a date.

"I think I'd prefer the date if I'm going to be honest," I tell Kato. If I am being truly honest, I'd have less of a chance of embarrassing myself if it was a sniper. Dating isn't high on my agenda; I have better things to do like learning three new languages so I can translate files for Aunt Magdalena. Even if I can see the appeal in his smile and height and those blue eyes, it's not like I could ever actually like him. He's my target.

"Can I pick you up at your house?" Kato asks with a smile. "Tonight maybe?"

"I live on an island, so picking me up there will be rather difficult. What if we meet at the ice cream shop in Phelps? Sweets, Treats and More?"

"I think I know the place. Home of the best ice cream flavor on the planet, right? You liked blue moon?"

"It was... the most flavorful thing I've ever tasted." It was amazing.

The smile on Kato's face grows. "Does two o'clock this afternoon work for you?"

I look down at my wrist. It's eleven in the morning. "Sure," I say. With any luck, he'll try to make a move, invite me to his house where I can survey the security system, and be back to Gangster Island in time to watch a movie with Marleen and her son.

"Okay, I will see you then."

"Okay." I nod. When I look up, he's still standing there, with that goofy smile on his face. "Uh, see you then, Kato," I say with the implication that the conversation is over.

"Right," he nods, and I watch him trip over a chair behind him as he makes for the doors. As soon as he leaves, I shake my head and can't help but smile. Yeah, there might be something wrong with me.

I walk through the rows of books to the checkout counter in the middle of the library. I place the book I want to borrow on the counter before fishing out my fake passport and the piece of mail that matches, saying I live in a house just out of town.

"Hello. Are you getting a card?" She holds out her hand for the ID.

I hand the fake and the piece of mail to her without a second thought.

The librarian takes my ID and hits a few buttons on her computer before looking up, her face scrunched in confusion. "Melissa?" she asks.

I nod. I like my fake name. Why is she questioning it?

"How long have you lived here?"

"Not long." Why is she questioning this? It's a library card, not airport security.

The librarian hands me a pink library card. "Just sign the back," she instructs about the card, and I do.

"Is that all?" I ask, placing the pen on the counter.

"So, you and Kato? Interesting pair, *Melissa*," she says, scanning my books again.

That's why she was giving me a weird look. She must have overheard. She knows I gave her a fake ID. And who uses a fake to get a library card?

"He's just showing me around since I'm new to these parts. Thank you." I hold out my hand for the book, hoping my already thanking her will push her to hand it over. Panic fills my throat. Can you get in trouble for using a fake to get a library card? At the very least, the small-town rumors of local, Kato, and a girl with a fake ID may start swirling. I can't look any more suspicious. She just needs to hand over the book. Of course, I'm never that lucky.

"You know I always thought he'd end up with the Millers' daughter. Anna something. Annalise? Anna Rose? Well, whatever it was, *she* was a real pretty thing."

"Okay," I say tersely. No, I did not miss the backhanded insult. "I haven't really met any pretty females around these parts. I really need to be going, though."

"Oh, all right. I'll see you around, okay, hun?" She finally hands me the book. I don't answer her as I make a beeline for the door, careful not to trip over the same chair Kato did.

RULE 10:

ONLY TRUST FAMILY.

The book isn't much help—a lot of boring facts about logging in a boring small lake town. The trees from here helped build Milwaukee and Chicago, *blah, blah, blah*, and then they all burned up in Chicago when a cow knocked over a lantern. I feel rather deflated, and the obligation to hang out with Kato this afternoon isn't helping my mood. My flip-flops kick up dirt around my bare ankles as I make my way to the ice cream shop, keeping a lookout out for my date.

I round the corner and the shop comes into view. Kato sits at one of the picnic tables, looking at his phone. I glance down at my watch. I'm five minutes early, and yet it looks like he's been waiting for a while.

I look back up, and since he's distracted by his phone, I take a moment to study him again. He sits with his feet flat on the ground. He's not worrying about his posture as he slumps forward toward the device. His hat blocks his view, a reason why most operatives don't wear baseball hats. Maybe his dad tells him not to wear a hat, and since he doesn't know his father's true line of work, he doesn't listen. He doesn't look trained. He looks like he would give soft hugs. That's a weird thing to note, but the longer I think about it, the truer it seems.

He looks up and spots me. My cheeks warm as if he could hear my hug thoughts. I'm being stupid again. He's my target. He's not just a teen boy; he's my target.

A smile spreads on his face. He jams his phone into his cargo shorts and stands, adjusting the black baseball cap on his head. He walks toward me.

I don't understand why he would wear a baseball cap and cover up his curly hair that he no doubt spends time and product on. But the thought doesn't stay in my head long—his hat isn't for a sports team. It's for the World Chess Championship and has little white chess pieces along the brim.

"Nice hat," I say as he comes up to me.

His lips curve up in that warm, funny half grin of his. "You play chess?"

I shrug. "I'm pretty good. How about you? Do you play or just watch?"

"Mostly watch. My mother was a huge fan, and she played all the time. Sometime you should show me how you play; we have this expensive board my mother played on daily before she passed away."

"I'm so sorry," I say and take a step closer to him, wanting to give him privacy surrounding such personal matters, if he wants it.

"Don't be. Everyone around here already has that covered." Kato removes his cap and, with his sly grin widening, plunks it down on my head. It's warm and obstructs my sightlines. "There. That looks way better on you, Ugly."

I smile despite myself as I straighten the hat on my head. "If you have lice and just gave it to me, I will kill you," I warn, the smile refusing to leave my face. What is it with boys giving me their hats?

Kato laughs and holds his arm out for me to take. "I swear I am lice-free."

"All right, Mr. Lice-Free, where are we off to this afternoon? Your place so I can cream you in chess?" I take his arm so he can lead the way. It would be rude not to, after all, and I can't be rude. I certainly can't be rude enough to scare him off.

"We are going to go to the Piggly Wiggly."

"The what?"

"The Piggly Wiggly! You know, 'Shop the Pig!'" Kato looks at me. I stare back as if he's lost his mind.

Shop the what? Piggly Wiggly?

"You've never been to a Piggly Wiggly?" he asks in disbelief.

"Are we going to an animal show?" Please say we're not going to an animal show. *Please say we are not going to an animal show.*

Kato bursts out laughing. "We are not. The Piggly Wiggly is a grocery store. I was thinking we pick up doughnuts. Then I know this sweet spot with a great view of South Twin Lake. It's near the Girl Scouts camp. We can go there and eat them and maybe talk or something."

"You could download chess on your phone, and I could destroy you," I offer. It would be much better if we took doughnuts back to his place so I could scope out his security system, avoid being murdered by his father, and be done with him and all of this. But eating doughnuts with a nice lake view and a possible easy chess win, well, I've never imagined such a pleasant mission.

Kato leads me on his arm to his silver truck and pops open the passenger door for me. For a moment, I just stand there unsure of my next move, but then I hoist myself up into the vehicle. The only piece of standard motherly advice I think I ever received growing up was a warning not to get into the vehicles of strangers. I suppose since he's the target, he's not technically a stranger. But unease still settles over me as the door closes.

"You look nervous," Kato observes, sliding into the driver's seat.

Am I really that obvious?

"There are no live pigs at the Piggly Wiggly, you know. Well, not normally," he teases, turning the key and bringing the truck to life.

I laugh. That's a normal response, right? "Just a lot on my mind," I say, trying to sound breezy.

"Okay. If you want to talk about anything, I've been told I'm a great listener."

"Okay, sure." I look out the window. The lake disappears behind trees and the road turns to dirt, dipping up and down and weaving left and right. I realize I have no idea how far it is from Phelps to the nearest Piggly Wiggly. If I was any good at counting seconds to keep track of how far we've traveled, I would start.

"You doubt my powers?" Kato teases and flashes that grin of his once more.

My heart flutters and I forget what we had been talking about. "What?"

"Never mind."

"How far is this Piggly Wiggly?" I ask.

Kato is silent for a moment before he speaks again. "You know if you don't want to go, that's fine. I can drop you back off at the docks. I didn't mean to pressure you into coming."

If I fail a mission because I can't go out on a date like a normal person, the fifth family could destroy my family. This isn't a hard mission, but the stakes are high. Not to mention, Quinton will never let me hear the end of it. I straighten up and look at Kato, trying to relax my face to hide the panic within. "Don't be silly," I say, straightening the hat on my head. "I want to go, okay? I'm just new at this."

"Going to grocery stores? Yeah, they're pretty crazy places."

"Oh, ha-ha. Most people don't take dates to grocery stores, you know."

Kato smiles as he slows down and veers wide to pass a deer standing on the side of the road, posed as though it might dart across at any moment. "Well, doughnuts are a tricky science. You know you got physics, chemistry, anatomy, earth science, and doughnuts. I wouldn't want to mess it up and get you a type of doughnut that you hate."

"That's very thoughtful of you."

"Well, thank you. I do try."

I tuck a piece of hair behind my ear. The only people I've met around my age are trained in espionage like I am. Even at their worst, they are more attentive to their surroundings than Kato is as he drives. He drives like he knows the land, as casual as a walk to the bathroom in your own home. He taps his fingers on the steering wheel like he has no idea that I could kill him twelve different ways before he could veer off the road. He really is just a clueless softy who likes me. He has no idea that his father would want me dead.

"You feeling all right? You haven't insulted me in like five whole minutes," Kato teases with a grin in my direction, one I return without even thinking.

"I just can't seem to figure you out, Kato," I respond, my voice not losing volume but gaining a softness.

"No?" He cocks one eyebrow up.

"No. Most of the time, you're this happy-go-lucky guy who seems to genuinely want to show me around and get me acclimated to Phelps, Conover, and the rest of the great northern-Wisconsin landscape, and then last night you act like taking out the trash was code for killing your dog or something."

"Oh." Kato's smile fades as his eyes bore into the road ahead.

"Oh?"

"Look, I'm sorry about last night. I shouldn't have just

bailed on you. My dad is very overprotective. He won't even let me ride my Harley anymore because he thinks it would be too easy to be snatched. It's hard, you know? For people like us, I mean."

I feel my heart rate spike. "People like us?"

"Yeah. You know, people with money. And, obviously, I would take these issues over what other people go through every day of the week. I'm not trying to say it's as hard for us as people without money, it's just—everyone has their troubles, you know? Our parents have a constant fear of us being kidnapped for a ransom. And it's not just our money. My grandmother, she was a victim of a brutal home invasion when she was a young woman. She instilled this fear and mentality into my dad of always looking over your shoulder; he's always so paranoid about my safety. I told him I was hanging out with a new friend today, and I barely got out without him insisting on coming along. Or running a hundred background checks on you. I'm sure your parents are the same way." Kato's laugh comes out forced. "Or maybe my dad is just crazy."

"Right. My parents are the same way because they're so rich and helicopter-y." I guess living on a private island in a large home would make me look rich, but all our money is stolen and it never felt like mine. It's not like I could ever go to the mall with the stolen crown jewels of Ireland and use them to pay for a fancy handbag. And I never see the money after it gets laundered. Still, I can play the role of a rich kid looking for a break from her parents. "It's like, I just want to live a normal life sometimes, you know?"

"Exactly!" The smile returns to Kato's lips. "My dad has me go by a different name every time we leave Wisconsin. And they're terrible names, too. I had the last name Butt the entire time we were in New York City last summer. What am I supposed to do with a name like Alex Butt?"

I let out a snort. That's truly horrible.

"You can laugh," Kato assures. "My dad, he thinks he's so

important that people would track him over state lines to take his son. No one has ever even tried anything even remotely like that. Just because my grandmother was robbed, doesn't mean there's people lining up to take us for ransom, you know?"

"The constant looking over your shoulder is tiring." It is. I know this from experience.

Kato nods. "I'm so glad I found someone who just gets it. This is nice."

Unfortunately, I do get it, and what's going on, better than he does. "Why were you guys in New York City?" I ask.

"Hm? Oh, my dad has an office near there that he tries to visit once a year or so. It's about a half hour north of the city. He keeps a lot of files there, and it's mostly just a nail-down-the-details type of operation. Real boring stuff," Kato explains.

Real boring unless you're racing out of it with a stolen file and security guards hot on your tail. "I think it's nice your dad takes you with him on his business trips."

"Your parents don't take you with them?"

"No." I shake my head and think of what I can say that won't reveal anything. "That's why I'm here without them. They're currently in Peru on business. I'm staying with family until they get back. It's supposed to just be for the summer, but we'll see."

"What part of Peru?" Kato asks, and the excitement in his voice makes it seem like Peru is a country he knows well.

"They're near the capital," I say. Rule nineteen: *confidence is key.*

"I've always wanted to go to Peru!"

"Really?" What are the chances of that? That means he's going to ask more questions that I don't have the answers to.

"I have always wanted to see Machu Picchu," Kato explains. "My dad said we could go once I graduate high school, but I'm not sure we'll be able to anymore."

89

"Why not?" I ask and move in the seat to fully face him.

"I don't know. He's just been acting weird recently. It's like something has happened, but he won't tell me what. He's been more protective than usual. And don't get me wrong, he's always been over the top, but I mean, it's been like he wants to wrap a bubble around me."

How strange is it that I know more about his father than he does? "I'm surprised your father let you go to the grocery store with me then."

"Well, he didn't want me to go at first. The whole background-check thing. But I told him who you are, you know, new to the area, and he thought it was nice of me."

"Well, I'll have to meet him sometime. Thank him in person." Abby's warning about keeping my distance from the man dances through my head. The most important thing is getting inside the house.

"Trust me, you don't want to," Kato says.

"Why not?"

"He's terrible with people. Worse than me."

"You're not bad with people." The compliment slips from my lips without even thinking about it. I must be getting better at this whole pretending-to-like-him thing. My mother is right, as much as I hate to admit it: the longer you're undercover, the easier it gets. "You're a really good person, Kato. Not every teenage boy would spend so much time helping someone get used to a new town without any ulterior motives."

Kato's mouth opens and closes without any noise coming out. A new type of smile forms on his lips, one that tells me there are ulterior motives. I just hope those motives are to take me back to his place and not to ruin my family.

"Thank you," he finally musters as we pass a sign to Darton's Twin Pine Resort. The hill dips once more. "We're almost to the store."

"Well, good, I'm excited to see this Piggly Wiggly and its

impressive selection of fresh doughnuts." When he doesn't respond, I look over at him and see his eyes fixated ahead at the road, his mouth a thin line. "What's wrong?"

"Nothing. It's just—nothing. Nothing is wrong."

"Okay, you're not very convincing, Kato." An expression like regret covers his face, and the panic swells back into my throat. Maybe I shouldn't have gotten in his truck. "We are going to the grocery store, right?"

"Yeah, of course," Kato assures, his cheeks reddening. The car falls to silence for the rest of the drive.

———

"IT'S JUST A GROCERY STORE," I say as I get my first look at "The Pig." The building is rectangular and built of whitewashed cinder blocks. Like any other grocery store I've seen. Gotta love the sign out front, though: a giggling pig wearing a white paper butcher's hat.

"Well, what did you think it was going to be?" Kato asks, noting the unimpressed look on my face.

I shrug and follow him inside past racks of fruit toward a pastry stand in the back.

As we get to a large wooden table full of plastic containers with melty doughnuts inside, he says, "My personal favorite is the chocolate-chip Danish. None of them are bad, though— except the lemon cake. Keep your stomach away from the lemon cake."

"What's wrong with the lemon cake?" Before he can answer, a display in my periphery catches my attention: To my left is a large selection of serious-looking paintball guns.

I went paintballing once on a family vacation. My parents bought a ghost town and taught us how to operate guns, as well as when to shoot to make sure you don't run out of ammo. It had been a fun trip—a real family vacation. Years later I learned we took family vacations because we were being pursued by assassins and had to go dark for a while. I wish it was as simple this time.

"Autumn?"

I turn at the warmth of Kato's hand placed gently on my arm.

A grin spreads on his lips, one I don't like but don't want to go away. "You want to play paintball?"

My smile matches his. "I thought you'd never ask."

RULE 11:

DON'T RELY ON TECHNOLOGY.

K ato drives us out to what looks like two stories of post-apocalyptic urban decay. Bright splats from errant shots polka-dot the building's peeling, gray exterior. A large sign declares, "WAR TO THE DEATH PAINTBALL STARTS EVERY HOUR!" Kato points it out as we park.

"Normally, there's a group that spends all day here. Every hour, everyone enters and has five minutes to spread out. Then there's an air horn and the last person to get shot wins. Got it?"

I nod my head. I haven't played in a while, but the stakes have never been lower. "So, we're against each other then?" That part I do like.

"We don't have to be. They call it a 'Hunger Games win' when two people or a team claim victory. They don't really care that much. Here, hold on." Kato turns off the truck and gets out, closing his door and coming around to open my side for me.

"You really don't have to do that," I say, hopping down.

"No, I don't have to, but I am a gentleman, so I insist," he says, and we walk in silence to the building.

At the counter inside, Kato puts down his dad's credit card.

A tattered vinyl couch sits in the front office, paint splatters pepper the walls, and Polaroids of past winners are pinned on a leader board. Judging by the dates on the pictures, it seems they hold a tournament the first Saturday of every month.

The door opens. I ignore the next people coming in. But then I hear a voice I recognize.

"That little girl is going to play? I might as well go home. I don't want to make her cry."

I bite my tongue and keep my head down to avoid blowing my cover. I'd know that voice anywhere. "I'm not so little," I protest after a moment of silence. He knows that.

"Ah, the little girl thinks she's tough. How cute," he says.

It takes every fiber of my being to hide my emotions.

I turn and my eyes land on that mop of red hair.

For some ungodly reason my brother is here, standing out like a lit torch. A guy about his age, who I recognize as a member of our security team, is with him. Quinton laughs. He is the only person I won't punch out for making a comment like that, because we both know I can outshoot him every day of the week. I'm also way too relieved to see him to be mad.

He's alive. He's here, and he's okay.

I want to run over, hug him, and then sock him in the shoulder and demand he tell me what the hell he is doing here and what the hell is going on. His presence either means my mission is over or he has managed to slip our parents and escape back to the States.

"Don't say that, man, come on," Kato defends my honor as he grabs two paintball rifles and two bags of paint off the table and comes to my side. He hands half of everything purchased to me.

"Look at that, Cinderella has a bodyguard," Quinton laughs as he places a hundred-dollar bill on the counter. The irony of his comment, seeing as I'm trained and Kato is not, is not lost on me. But I know Kato doesn't get it as his face begins to twist in anger.

"I think Cinderella's bodyguard is getting angry," Bruce says.

"Come on, Kato, we'll beat them in the game," I say as I try to pull Kato away from my brother.

"Yeah, I look forward to taking them out," Kato says with a light laugh that lacks all humor—it makes me smile. He is so protective of me when I could literally kill everyone here without breaking a sweat. Well, I would break a sweat fighting Quinton; we are evenly matched.

"Bulldog here is going to be let off his chain in there! Watch out, Bruce!" Quinton declares, slapping his guard/buddy in the gut.

"Oh no! I'm so scared!" Bruce mocks in a high-pitched voice. Both boys make barking sounds like dogs.

It takes all my strength not to start laughing.

"Hey, Bulldog, how about you tell your girlfriend to go wait in the car? We don't want to embarrass you when you get out in the first ten minutes," Bruce laughs.

"Come on, guys, we're all here for a good time, okay?" I say, pulling my lips up to hide my true feeling as I pretend to mess with my gun.

"Actually, we're here to win," Quinton says and takes a step, so he stands right in front of me. "Is that a problem, Cinderella?"

"Well, seeing as how *we're* going to win, yeah, I'd say that's a problem—for you," I challenge back, and my brother takes a threatening step closer.

"Hey-hey!" Kato steps in, shoving Quinton away from me. "Back off, dude. I'm not going to ask again."

Quinton and Bruce burst out laughing and make more obnoxious dog noises. It's nice to see my brother laughing so much. It's nice to just *see* my brother. I'm still worried about him, about my family and my mission. But I feel better having him right in front of me. Maybe I won't be such a mission screw up if he's here.

"He's not going to ask again!" Quinton howls like a dog. "What's pretty boy gonna do?" Quinton challenges, this time stepping closer to get in Kato's face.

"Back off," Kato says.

"No, I'd rather see what you can do." His smile fades, and he jabs Kato in the shoulder with his hand as he talks. "You think you're so great? So tough? Mr. Big Shot coming after me?" My brother's voice isn't teasing anymore.

"Don't fight in my lobby," the guy behind the counter interjects with as much enthusiasm as a gate-change announcement at the airport.

"He's right," Kato says. "The session is about to begin, and we look forward to destroying you. Come on, Autumn."

"Autumn?" My brother echoes, his jerk façade dropping at Kato's uttering of my real name. With his disapproving look, he reminds me with his eyes. *Rule three: never use your real name.* My first mission on my own and already I have disappointed one of my family members. "What a dumb name," Quinton adds before growling and barking again to cover his near misstep.

"You guys are jerks." I turn and grab Kato's arm, pulling him toward the door into the paintball arena. The clock is ticking down to zero.

I FIRE off two rounds to the floor below. Kato's knowledge of the place had come in handy when we entered the abandoned-looking structure. It's not possible to get to the higher ground in five minutes, but Kato knew a back staircase that gets us to the fourth floor—while my brother and Bruce are two floors down. They scramble up the main stairs that loops around the large opening through the center of the building.

I rain paintball hell down on them.

"You're really good at this," Kato comments.

It's Quinton who is really good. We are about twenty minutes into our hour-long open play slot, and he and Bruce have knocked out all the other competitors.

"Thanks."

Bruce moves into my view, and I fire twice. Both hit him square in the back. That leaves Quinton against me and Kato.

"Just the redhead left, and we win."

"Okay," Kato nods. "Can I do anything?"

"I got it," I assure him and flash a smile before focusing back on finding Quinton. "So, what happens when we win?" I ask as I watch the main staircase for my brother to step into view. I count the seconds. He must be getting closer, but I can't detect his silent footsteps. Bruce had lumbered, his footsteps giving him away, but Quinton is better trained and won't make a mistake like that.

"The winners take a minute and sign their name on a wall. When it's a 'Hunger Games win,' though, the winning team goes all the way up to the roof. They have as much time as is left on the clock; so, you know, they hang out and take selfies and stuff."

"Hang out?" I repeat as I scan for any sign of my brother, losing count of his supposed steps.

"Yeah. You know. 'Couple' things."

A flash of red hair catches my eye, and I fire once, purposely to the left of my target.

"Did you get him?" Kato asks.

"Yeah, I think so." I lie with a nod. "He's out."

Kato breaks into a wide grin and shoulders his gun. "That was amazing! We won! If you want—"

I fire once more and shoot Kato in the leg before he can finish his sentence, causing him to scream out, either in pain or surprise or both, I don't know. I don't want to do any "couple" things with him; I want him gone so I can talk to my brother. "Sorry, Kato, but this isn't 'The Hunger Games.'

There can only be one winner," I say and shoot him in the other leg as well.

He stares at me in disbelief.

"I win," I add after a moment, for no reason.

"What the hell is wrong with you?" Kato asks. "We were working as a team!"

"I'll meet you downstairs," I say, unsure what else to say. He is right. We had been working as a team, and we had been getting along really well. And then I shot him, the guy I needed to convince to trust me enough to take me to his house. Suddenly the weight of my split-second choice comes crashing down on my head.

"Okay. Well, you have fun alone at the top," Kato scoffs, turning and stomping away from me.

After a few moments, I hear the firing of a paintball gun below me. I assume Quinton has taken out Kato as well. The Alderidge siblings spared no expenses hurting that guy today. A twinge of guilt pricks me, and I can't bat it away. At least not until I hear my brother behind me.

"So, we meet again, Cinderella."

"What are you doing here?" I whip around and ask in a whisper-roar.

"I'm so glad there are cameras everywhere around here, so I can get your face on video when you lose," Quinton says, and I roll my eyes. He acts like I haven't seen the security feed on the worker's computer, too. There are cameras everywhere. Everywhere, I realize, except the roof behind the stairs enclosed in cement. I turn and bolt, heading up the stairs for the roof. Quinton takes off behind me, no longer worrying about the sound his feet make as he follows me up; he calls out how dead I'm going to be when we get to the top.

I burst open the door to the roof, tear around the corner, and duck behind the stairs. It's not wide, but the roof extends behind it, leaving me plenty of space for shelter or a shootout. The camera faces the front of the stairs, so everything beneath the steps is hidden. Quinton tears around the corner, and I grab him by the arm, spinning him around into a hug, his gun digging into my side.

"I missed you," I say, and he tears himself away from me. We're not exactly the hugging type of family. "Where have you been? What is going on?" I demand.

And that's when my eye catches something out of place. I inhale sharply.

"Quinton..."

"What? We're fine, really, I'm just back to—" I grab his left hand in both of mine and he asks, "Hey, what are you doing?"

On my brother's ring finger is none other than a ring. And not just some cheap costume-jewelry ring—a wedding ring.

"Oh. That." Quinton appears embarrassed as he pulls his hand away from me. "Right. I was supposed to leave that in the car. Mr. Thindrel wanted me to leave it, so I wouldn't lose it. Apparently, it's a family heirloom. I guess I forgot. It's worth, like, twenty grand."

"You're married?!"

"No, not yet. Engaged. I guess you could say it's a promise ring? Whoever marries into their family is the one who wears the engagement ring, which would be me, so I'm wearing one and she's not. Although it will be my wedding ring. But that's not why I'm here. Autumn, look, we don't have a lot of time. You need to come home. Ashlynn will take over here with your target. You need to get to Russia."

"Wait, you said Mr. Thindrel? Why would he be involved with your ring?"

Quinton rubbed the back of his neck, as if to hide the ring behind his head. "Autumn, I'm engaged to Naomi Thindrel."

"You're what?!"

"I'm engaged to Naomi—"

"I heard you, you moron! Why are you engaged to Naomi Thindrel? What about Abby?"

"That's not what matters right now." Quinton shoulders his

paintball gun and refuses to look me in the eye. "You need to get to Russia. How long will it take you to pack?"

"I'm not going to Russia. I'm not going anywhere."

Quinton finally meets my gaze, a glare in his eyes as if I had just called him something far worse than moron. "Mom and Dad sent me to take you to Russia. They want me to meet with Dimitri as well. We can't blow your cover when we head downstairs. You're going to figure out a way to ditch your date and then we're going back to Uncle's house, grabbing your crap, and leaving."

"No." I cross my arms, not breaking his gaze. "I'm not failing my first solo mission. And I'm not leaving this rooftop until you tell me what happened."

"Why are you so stubborn?"

"Why are you engaged?!"

"You think I want to be, Autumn? You think after we got home, I thought, 'Yeah, I'll go propose to a girl I met once because that sounds like a jolly good time!' Our family is going dark around the globe. We are losing everyone; our resources are going up in smoke. You're too close to the cause. We're evacuating Wisconsin as soon as Ashlynn gets the intel."

"But it's my—"

"And, yes, Ashlynn, because she is not third in line to take over this family and her getting engaged to someone would not help us. As soon as I marry Naomi, we have the full support and resources of the Thindrels. Do you get that?"

"How does that have anything to do with me going to Russia?"

"As soon as you marry Dimitri, we have the same from the Daxterovs. We need to stay above water, and for that we need to cement relations. The easiest way to do that is through marriage: mine to Naomi and yours to Dimitri."

"Wait, you want me to go to Russia and get engaged? I'm not old enough. I'm only seventeen." Now I feel not only my first solo mission slipping away but my freedom.

"It doesn't matter anymore."

"It matters to me."

"How are you not getting the severity of what is happening? If we keep going downhill at the speed we're going, we are three months short of being wiped out by the fifth family."

The fifth family. My mouth goes dry. "Kato—"

"If that's even his real name. Smart agents use fake names."

Whether intended or not, his comment hits me like a slap across the face. I am smart. I have been training for this my entire life. It is a lot different in the real world versus training with Dad and Quinton.

"He's not an agent. He's just a dumb boy with a really evil dad."

Quinton shakes his head. "I don't trust him, especially not with you. It doesn't matter, though; you're coming with me."

"No, I'm not."

"Dammit, Autumn, we need to go."

"So, what are you going to do? Kidnap me? Not even you can make me marry someone."

Quinton runs a hand over his tired face. He looks older, not in the wise, mature way but in the no-longer-gets-enough-sleep and worries-all-the-time way. "Please, Autumn, if he turns on you, which he is going to do as soon as he thinks he has everything he can get out of you, he will kill you. You need to come with me."

"We don't even know he's a part of what his father is doing. I've been the one spending time with him. He isn't like us. He clearly has no training. It's not his fault who his dad is. He's not involved."

"We don't know that he's not!" A flash of fear crosses my brother's face before he stifles it. He is better at hiding his emotions than I remember. Or, perhaps he has never hidden them from me before.

"I know," I assure.

"You need to come with me, Autumn," he presses.

"We both know I'm not going to do that willingly. This is my mission. Thank you, for your concern, but I need you to trust me that I can handle this."

Quinton nods. "Mom and Dad are going to be livid with me when I come back without you."

"I told Kato they were in Peru."

"Peru? Why?"

"It was the first country that came to mind that wasn't where you guys were."

Quinton shakes his head and rolls his eyes. "No way Kato bought that, Autumn. We don't have any bases in South America."

"Well, he didn't challenge it if that's what you're insinuating. He just asked questions about Peru. I don't think he's as much a part of this, whatever this is, as you think. I get the feeling he really doesn't like his dad and has been kept in the dark."

Quinton narrows his eyes. "What are you suggesting?"

"He trusts me, not Ashlynn. If we switch roles and then something happens, there will be no keeping Ashlynn's cover. If you ask Mom and Dad—"

"Fine." Quinton purses his lips. "But this is your birthday gift, buttsnot."

I make a pouting face at my brother. "I want one more thing for my birthday, Dorito dust."

"Yeah? What's that?"

Before he can react, I raise my paintball gun and shoot him twice in the chest, bright teal splashing up and staining his chin as well as his shirt. "When we get downstairs, I'm clearly the winner."

He takes a step back and smears the paint with his hand. "You're damn lucky you're my sister." He lunges at me, paint fingers forward, as he tries to wipe them off on me.

I let out a squeal as I dodge away from him, but with the

element of surprise, he's faster. This is typical Quinton behavior. Get the paint on me, make us both losers just a little bit. Happy losers.

My brother grabs me in a headlock and stops an inch from wiping the paint on my face. He sighs and lets go of me. "If it looks like we had fun, your cover is blown."

Oh. Right.

"I'll follow you back downstairs." The air shifts back to being heavy.

We climb downstairs. Bruce stands behind the counter, messing with wires. Static dances across the monitors that had been displaying footage from inside the facility. The front desk employee running the place glares down at Bruce.

"I said I was sorry! I tripped!" Bruce doesn't sound like it was his first time apologizing. Quinton's bodyguard, despite leaving my brother alone, had managed to give us privacy. We wouldn't have had to hide so well to keep our cover.

Quinton leaves me in the doorway and goes over to Bruce, grabbing the boy by the collar and hauling him to his feet. "Let's go."

"Hey!" Bruce replies. "Did you win?"

Kato sees me and comes over.

Quinton looks down at his teal-stained shirt and then back at Bruce like Bruce is an idiot. "What do you think? Let's go."

"Hang on," Bruce says and pulls something out of his pocket, reattaching it to the nest of wires. I don't think anyone sees him grab the device except me. Whatever it is, it instantly brings all the screens back up.

"We lost sight of you. I was worried," Kato says and places his hands on my arms. I tear my gaze from my brother and look up at the boy who's still looking at me like I am the world. "Before all the footage went down, I saw the guy start chasing you, but then we couldn't see or hear anything. I was really worried." He lowers his voice. "That guy seems like the kind you would want to avoid."

Thank you, Bruce, I think. "I'm fine, Kato. I'm sorry I shot you."

"I'm just glad you're okay." Kato rubs my arms before he continues, "And I kind of liked it. Shows your competitive side. Speaking of which, I want a rematch."

I give a small laugh. That's what the flirty girls in the books always do. A small laugh and a brush of the hair behind the ear. My hair is already behind my ear, though, so I can't do that. "A rematch? Yeah, I don't have any paint on me, so I guess I can go beat you again."

"I'm thinking laser tag this time."

"Laser tag?"

"Have you played before?"

I am about to answer when Quinton cuts us off, yelling as he leaves. "I'll see you in Hell, Cinderella!" He and Bruce start up with the barking noises again until the door closes, cutting off their last words. Or grunts.

"That guy is really starting to get on my nerves," I comment, though my brother tends to reside primarily on my nerves.

"Did you ever catch what his name was?" Kato asks.

"No," I lie. How much *does* Kato know?

Kato takes my hand in his, leading me outside. As the door to the paintball arena slams shut behind us, he freezes. "We didn't get your picture," he says.

"Well, that's okay," I assure. "I don't need a picture on the wall to remember this day."

"No, it's not okay." Kato lets go of my hand, pulling his phone from his pocket. "You won, that means you get your picture taken." Kato holds his phone up, and snaps a zillion pictures, turning it at different angles. I burst out laughing; all my nerves, all my stress, all my anxieties bubbling over into a fit of laughter at getting my photo taken like he's paparazzi.

"No," I say and move toward him as he snaps another one. I tug on his arm holding the phone. "Come on, you have to be in it too. I hate photos of just me, but I can tolerate photos of me with other people."

Kato grins and switches his phone camera to selfie mode as he strings his free arm around my waist, pulling me close to him. I smile up at us. We look like a real couple. I wish we were.

"Okay, say cheese," Kato requests, and I do. "Okay, now say I just shot the guy who bought me a doughnut!"

I try to glare at him but fail as he makes a silly face at me, making me grin, which makes him laugh.

"I like winning," I mutter, but neither of our smiles fade.

"I know. I'll have a welt on my leg for a week to prove it."

I give him a playful shove as he takes another photo of us.

AUTUMN

AGE 12

"*Sometimes being silent is the best way to get information out of someone who is untrained,*" Mother said. *She was teaching me my lesson while Quinton and Dad were on a practice mission without me.*

"*Why couldn't I have gone with Quinton?*" *I asked, a sour look on my face.* "*He's always going out training and learning how to use weapons and stuff, and I've barely been trained how to have quiet feet! All I seem to be taught is how to mess with people's heads.*"

My mother studied me.

I sat on the couch in the living room, my feet tucked up under me as I leaned on the velvet armchair. A book my mother wanted me to finish yesterday on women's etiquette that could've been written in the 1600s lay open in my hands.

"*When people see your brother, they'll see an aggressive boy, someone physically dangerous. They won't give him the time to talk; they'll simply take him out. When people see you, they'll see someone they can use to get information. And that's not your fault, nor is it Quinton's. It's the world's fault.*"

"*Because I'm a woman? Is that why I'm reading this stupid book?*"

"*When was that book written?*"

"*What?*" *I left one finger on the page I was on, closed the book, and inspected its hard blue cover. The book appeared to be in good shape. "I don't know," I muttered as I turned open the cover, looking for the copyright. When I saw it, my mouth fell open. "It says it was written last year."*

"It was."

"Someone seriously published this last year?"

"They did. Which is why you are reading it. People see a thin blonde girl and jump to the conclusion that you're not deadly."

"By not training me, though, aren't we proving them right?"

My mother pulled a knife out of her belt and threw it at my head.

I moved just as the blade whizzed past my ear.

My eyes went wide.

I jumped up on the couch and struck a firm balance, my knees bent, my feet in place.

Mother pulled out another knife and threw it.

I moved the book directly in the path of the blade and jumped down to the floor. The knife embedded itself into the book. I pulled it out and flipped back over the couch, taking cover.

I threw the knife back, my aim sure. Slow to get out of the way, the knife ripped my mother's shirt. Its handle stuck into the fireplace mantel behind her, scarring the reclaimed barnwood.

"Autumn," my mother said, her voice calm and level as always. "You are deadly. You just don't give yourself the necessary credit. You will be fully trained. But right now, it's more important that you learn to take the misperceptions people have about you and exploit them. Now, come sit."

RULE 12:

KEEP YOUR EMOTIONS IN CHECK.

"Are you okay?" Kato asks as we drive. We've been on the road for about ten minutes, and I have yet to say anything, so I suppose the question is justified.

Kato keeps pointing a concerned look over at me. With his mop of hair, he is kind of cute, the longer you look at him. His eyes are a clear crystal blue, like a glassy, undisturbed lake, and he has the most defined eyelashes I have ever seen on a guy who isn't wearing mascara.

Okay, fine, he's handsome.

Not that it matters, I remind myself.

I focus on what my brother said. Mom and Dad want me to marry Dimitri as soon as possible. Although he seems nice it isn't like I am the stereotypical girl in those old romance novels blown away at first glance and planning my wedding.

Dimitri is handsome, too, but in a different way from Kato. Where Kato is clean cut, Dimitri wears his hair ruffled so it hangs out of his hat at all angles. Kato communicates more through expressions and gestures, and his hands move when he gets excited, which is rather adorable. Dimitri, on the other hand, is more poised when he speaks, and uses more charming language, even though English isn't his native tongue. I can only guess that under all those layers of woolen clothing, he is in better shape than Kato due to his family upbringing. He probably would have just as many women after him if he lived a lifestyle like Kato's. Of course, as my fiancé, it wouldn't matter.

"Autumn?" he asks again, and I realize I haven't answered. "Autumn, you're starting to freak me out."

"Oh, sorry, I'm fine," I say.

"Okay, good." Kato breathes easier as his gaze turns back to the road. "Did that red-headed guy say something to you in there? You seem a little freaked. And you keep staring at me. Not that I mind you staring at me or anything. I kind of like it, actually." He flashes me a teasing, flirty smile that shows off his straight, white teeth.

"No, I'm fine," I assure. Kato's right, though, I am freaked. I have long known that eventually I will marry Dimitri and move to Russia, but it isn't supposed to be anytime soon. "Eventually" was always so far away. Now it's as soon as I complete my mission.

If Quinton can marry Naomi for the family, I can do my part. But I won't fail this assignment.

Kato focuses on the side of the road where a deer watches us pass by.

The drive is another twenty minutes before he slows the truck and eases it into the parking lot in front of Northern Lights Laser Tag. Sometimes silence is the best weapon, but I know being silent this entire ride doesn't help my objective. Kato didn't try to fill the silence, either—no matter how awkward. He asked if I was okay a few times throughout the ride, but he was comfortable being with me in silence.

What misperceptions does this boy have about me? After today, I bet he thinks of me as uptight and rude more than anything. No one wants to hang out with uptight and rude people.

And what misperceptions might I have about him?

When Kato comes over and opens the door for me, I give him a smile. "Thank you."

"Thank you?" Kato chuckles. "You must feel really bad about shooting me."

"Sure, that's it." I try to sound playful. I need to be more relaxed. Quinton said three months. That's not much time, yet it's way more time than I want to spend in Wisconsin. But I don't want to lose Kato. Or this mission to Ashlynn. Not anymore.

"I'm going to beat you at laser tag," he says, nudging me with his shoulder as we walk together to the building.

"In your dreams," I retort. I may never have played laser tag before, but I am skilled with firearms and dodging weapons. I can even snatch knives out of the air about fifty percent of the time. Lasers can't be that much harder, right?

Kato holds the door open.

"Now who's being suspiciously polite?" I tease, walking ahead of him to the counter to pay the guy. Kato grabs us both vests and hands me mine. The laser gun is attached to it with a black flexible wire and slides into a holster on the side. I zip my vest and pull the laser gun out. I bounce it in my hand a couple times, weighing it, finding its balance. It's so light. It feels unnatural.

Kato leads us to a small room outside the arena. We have to watch a short video first. A teenage boy Kato must know from high school goes over safety like no running, no spitting, no throwing other kids, no tackling, no physical touching of any kind.

"Are we on the same team?" I whisper to Kato, leaning into him so he can hear me. My back presses against his arm as I do, and warmth fills my cheeks. He's still listening to instructions and doesn't appear phased by the proximity.

"Technically. Though we were last time, too, remember." He casts a look down at me and his gaze falls on my lips. Our mouths are a lot closer to each other than they should be. I tear my gaze from his lips.

Focus. I need focus. I need to stop fixating on how close we are. I straighten up so I'm not touching him anymore. "You're going to try and shoot me as soon as we get in there, aren't you?"

The devilish grin he shoots back answers my question. I raise my hand. The high school boy explaining the course stops talking and looks at me in confusion. "You have a question?"

"Yes. Can I shoot him now?" I throw Kato a smirk, which he returns.

"No," the guy says, like duh, I should know that. "You shouldn't shoot your teammate at all, but the lasers don't work out here. There's thirty seconds delay after you're let in before it starts—so you have a chance to run away from her, Kato."

Kato shakes his head. "I don't think I'm going to run."

"Great." The high school boy does not care. He finishes his scripted speech then opens the door for us.

Kato grabs my hand, and I look at him in surprise. He pulls me after him into the dark. His gun is holstered; mine is in my hand.

"Shh," he whispers, darting through the darkness. He clearly knows the course and moves behind a pair of pillars toward the back where we're hidden. The scuffles of others hurrying about in the arena and the sounds of laser shots surround us. Like old *Star Trek* sound effects, the echoing "pew-pews" are comical compared to the blasts and explosions that I'm accustomed to of real guns.

"Kato, what are you doing?" I whisper.

"Making the most of my thirty seconds before I kill you. Or, more likely, you kill me." Kato walks me back into the dark corner, his suit blocking mine from laser fire should anyone sneak up on us.

"Seriously, Kato, what are you doing?" I ask again, my heart rate quickening. His body presses against mine in the dark. "Something I should have done a while ago," he whispers, his lips so close to mine, each word brushes against my skin. I don't know what's wrong with me, but in this moment, it's like my mind betrays me. Every instinct in me screams that kissing the target during a situation with guns, even if they are just laser guns, is a bad idea—a poor choice.

"Even after I shot you?" I ask, and his lips meet mine in the dark. This is what I should be doing, right? I should be getting close to him.

I close my eyes and lean into him, pulling him closer. His hand slides against my cheek as he presses me against the wall. His lips move against mine. His strong arms draw me closer until I can smell the woodsy scent of campfire on him. The fingers of my free hand move up into his soft hair and wrap around his locks. I drop my gun and place my other hand on his vest.

And then I hear a screeching, high-pitched techno sound from my vest. A light vibration skitters across my chest. I shove Kato away and see his gun pressed against me. My jaw drops, and the sense of weightlessness from a moment before vanishes, replaced by surprise and rage.

"You shot me!" I exclaim.

"Now we're even," he says with a smirk that takes all my strength not to slap off.

"You shot me!"

"Yeah, you said that already."

I grab the cord on my fallen weapon and flip the gun up into my hand with a speed and skill that surprises even me. I shoot him back.

My vest stops blinking, and Kato shoots me again, which reignites it.

"You jerk!" I yell, but a laugh sneaks out.

"Shh," he says, though he is laughing, too. He takes a step back closer to me. "There are other people in here, Autumn."

I shoot him again, and he stops moving closer.

"Well, now, that's just uncalled for."

"Really?" I say with a grin.

We remain hidden behind the pillars, and the sight of them reminds me of hiding in the paintball arena earlier today with Quinton. The reason I'm here, returns like a snow squall to my mind. I'm supposed to go to Russia. I'm supposed to get married. I'm not supposed to be kissing my cute target in laser tag and having a good time.

My smile fades. My first kiss would always be this. I'll never have a real first kiss. Mine will always be part of a mission. It's not my own. Sadness ripples through me. My eyes sting at the threat of tears, and I'm grateful it's dark in here so Kato can't see them. I need to get my emotions in check, and fast. And so, I shut off my feelings like my mother taught me.

"You okay?" Kato moves closer, brushing hair from my face. Is it that obvious I'm not okay? The sting in my eyes is gone, but he saw a shred of my vulnerability. Again, my mother would be so disappointed.

"Yeah, I just want to leave," I whisper.

"Do you want me to take you home?" he asks, taking a step away from me, as if he is worried that he is the issue.

"No!" I shout more quickly than intended. "I don't want to go home." I'm sure my uncle has been told that Quinton has come to collect me for a wedding. I know what is waiting for me on Gangster Island. Ashlynn will pressure me into leaving so she can have the mission. My uncle will yell at me and say I have broken protocol by telling Quinton to give me more time. And Marleen will be waiting with a wedding binder, excited to start making plans I don't want to make. I want to be a normal teenage girl. I want to be able to hang out with Kato because he is a nice, cute boy who likes me. I want to kiss him without feeling guilty or because it's part of a mission.

But I am engaged to Dimitri.

My family needs me in Russia.

And I need to know Kato's home security.

"Okay," Kato takes a step back closer. "You want to go eat doughnuts then?"

A smile spreads back over my face. "More than anything."

RULE 11:

CHECK THE BACKSEAT.

"We're here," Kato says, bringing the truck to a stop on the gravel shoulder at the side of the road. I can't see anything except the thick woods that are all around us and a narrow, trampled-down path through the trees to my right.

"Where?" I ask. "Why do I get the feeling this is where you dump the bodies?"

Kato laughs like I'm joking. "I'm not an amateur, Autumn." I like his teasing voice. "You have to dump dead bodies in the lake! Here my dates might stumble across them."

He reaches into the backseat to grab the doughnuts we picked up from the Piggly Wiggly before he gets out and hurries around to my side of the truck to open my door. He holds his hand out for me. I give him a smile, allow myself to take his hand, and hop out of the vehicle. He closes the doors and locks them before jamming the keys into his pocket. "It's a little bit of rough terrain to get to the spot," he warns.

"I'll be fine," I assure. I deal with rough terrain on most training and team missions. My shoes are outfitted with extra traction, a specialty type my cousin in Milan invented and produced for the whole family. I may not have the softest feet, or the quickest, but most of the time I have balance and am sure-footed.

"I was just thinking, if you need a hand or anything..." Kato trails off as he makes his way to the path. "Never mind."

Does he mean he wants to hold hands? I'm not much of a hand-holder. My parents stopped holding my hand in public as soon as I could walk on my own. Once, I wandered off in a grocery store and when my mother got me home, she taught me how to track someone in a public space and how to avoid a tail. I was like six. She could have just held my hand.

I follow Kato through the trees, and we make our way uphill. He trips more than once. Every time his foot slips, I worry I will have to catch him to keep him from sliding into me and spilling the doughnuts.

A grin comes to my lips as we make our way, the sadness from earlier dissipated. A walk through nature with a cute boy. I don't think I've ever gone out in nature for the joy of it without it being an exercise or turning into one. Once I thought my family was going on a camping trip, but it turned out my parents left Quinton and me alone in the woods without any supplies, except a small canteen of water, for three days so they could assess our reactions and performance. I was twelve. Quinton had just turned fifteen. Careful surveillance was in place, and we were never in any real danger—not that we knew that.

"How far is it?" I call.

"You getting tired already?" Kato calls back, flashing a quick glance behind him.

I haven't even broken a sweat. But would an untrained girl be getting tired? "A little."

"Well, don't worry. It's just a little farther."

"Sounds great!" Something about his voice makes my brows furrow. He sounds out of breath. The quality of his voice is different, with a different tone, a different accent. I shake my head and remind myself of my intel. The guy is from

Wisconsin. His voice is just his voice. My mind is playing tricks on me. "Hey, Kato, did you bring any water?" I call up, wanting to hear his voice again, to see if I can catch it.

"No, sorry."

There it is again. Just slightly. When he is tired, he sounds different. Does everyone sound different when they're tired? I suddenly can't remember if people do.

It doesn't matter what his voice sounds like. It won't change that he is my target, or that I need to get inside his house, or that I am using him to further my family and take down his. I will leave him without a word of goodbye and marry Dimitri as soon as this is over.

A pang of guilt hits me in the gut. I try to ignore it.

My mind goes to our moment together at laser tag when he pressed me against the wall and leaned down, his lips connecting with mine. The look on his face just before we kissed was a look of happiness and admiration.

And here I am, using him.

"You still doing okay back there?" Kato calls.

"Yes, thank you!" I call back and silently curse myself. I sound so formal. Kato glances back at me with a smile. He holds out his hand for me to take. "I'm doing fine," I assure him. The last step up rises a lot higher than the step below. I stop. I look at Kato to take his hand but notice he is shimmering with sweat. I would rather fall down the hill than grab a sweaty hand. "Thank you, though," I add and grab the ledge, hoisting myself up with ease. Kato struggles up after me.

As we come out of the trees, we step onto a rock ledge, looking down and over the hilly Wisconsin Northwoods, a shimmering blue lake in the distance. As though Kato ordered it, an eagle swoops overhead, its wings outstretched, riding the breeze, its black eyes scanning the forest floor for food.

"Beautiful, right?" he asks, his gaze taking in the sight.

He calls this beautiful? This is stunning and breathtaking.

He calls me beautiful, too. How can I be described with the same word as this?

"It's perfect," I say softly. Kato plops down in the dirt and opens the plastic bag, the face of a pig on one side, its curling pig tail on the other. He pulls out the melty, chocolate-topped baked goods we had picked out together. I ease myself down next to him. For a while, we sit in silence and eat; awestruck by nature, just existing with the rolling green and blue hues. The eagle, in the distance now, glides against a backdrop of forest and wildflowers.

I guess this is what I am supposed to be doing, but something in me still screams it's wrong. My family is fighting to survive. Quinton said three months. And to help, here I am sitting outside basking in the warm weather eating doughnuts with a cute boy. Guilt gnaws at me in more ways than one. And what I picked up in Kato's voice still doesn't sit well with me. What if I'm wrong about him? The voices in my head get louder when I look over at Kato, and he's looking at me the way a pirate looks at gold coins. I smile back.

Kato leans closer and panic rises in me when I realize he is going in for a kiss. On instinct, I lean away. I don't know why. It's not like we didn't kiss earlier in the day, and it's not like I didn't enjoy it. It had been nice, even if he did only kiss me so he could shoot me. That bit of trickery was my favorite part—totally something I would do.

"Sorry, I just—" Kato pulls back and rubs the back of his neck. "I'm sorry, Autumn, that was stupid of me. I don't want to ruin this. Just forget it happened."

I lean over and give him a kiss on the cheek. He looks over at me, but embarrassment darkens his features. I can't push him away. There's too much at stake. I grab at the back of his head and pull him to me, kissing him with all the awkwardness of my inexperience. As he kisses back, the air leaves my lungs. All the thoughts in my head disappear.

They crash back in as he pulls away, my head moving with

him at first, my lips trying to follow his, before the kiss is broken. He leans back toward me and presses his forehead against mine as we sit there. I want to kiss him again, to pull him back to me, to have our lips meet once more. I want to hold him close and forget the world, forget the danger, forget my mission. I just want to be here, in this moment, with him. And I want to enjoy it. But I don't have the luxury to fall for him. I have a mission, and I need to stop pretending I don't.

"If you don't want to kiss me, I didn't mean to pressure you," he says, a smile on his lips. I know he can tell by looking at me that isn't the case.

"Shut up," I whisper against his lips before I kiss him again, pressing myself against him. That giddy, mind-blanking, breathless feeling returns.

Kato wraps his arms around me, guides me onto my back, and continues kissing me. He slides a knee on either side of me. The last time I was flat on my back with someone kneeling over me, I kneed him in the groin and nearly shoved him off a rooftop during a birthday training mission. Today, my hands wrap tightly around Kato's neck, but I use them to draw him closer so more of his body presses against mine.

After a moment, he pulls away and looks down at me with such joy. I've never kissed anyone like this before. I wonder if he has.

It takes a jarring second for me to remind myself that I'm not a foolish girl out on a date kissing a boy. I still need him to take me back to his place so I can examine his security system.

Gently, I place a hand on Kato's chest. He lets me guide him off me so that we're lying side by side. I move my face next to his ear, feeling his warm breath against my ear and hair. "Could we take this back to your place?" I whisper, hoping I'm as seductive sounding as I think.

"No." Kato moves away from me, shaking his head. "I

mean, my dad wouldn't like it if I brought someone back to the house."

"Oh."

"I do still have the truck, though, if you want to, uh—"

Crap, now I've shot myself in the foot. "What time is it getting to be?" I ask, not letting him finish his sentence. I pull my phone from my pocket, sit up, and move away from him. "Oh, jeez, I really should be going here."

"Yeah, of course," Kato says with a sheepish grin. If I wasn't as trained as I am, I may not have noticed his slight change in posture—he's relieved. Is it strange I feel a twinge in my gut when I see his relief? "Do you want a ride to the docks?" Kato offers.

Part of me does. We're on South Twin Lake, and Phelps and the boat are at the other end of North Twin Lake. Though I'm tired, I'm not getting in his truck after his last comment. I shake my head. "That's okay. I like the fresh air," I lie. I hope I'm not getting in over my head with this boy.

RULE 14:

GUNS ONLY CAUSE MORE ISSUES.

> Hey I had fun today ☺ What are you doin tomorrow?

I read the text from Kato again as I sit under the window in my room. The lights are off. A patch of moonlight provides enough light as I decide what to write back.

I usually don't text much. Most messages I get are instructions, which I answer and then delete. But I don't want to delete this one. Perhaps it will be helpful to keep Kato's texts as reference.

My thumbs hover over the keys. The glowing screen stares blankly back up at me. I have tapped it twice to keep it from going dark due to inactivity.

> I had fun too

I hit send before I can think twice about it. I bite my lower lip and wait for his response, rereading what he wrote. I realize I have forgotten to tell him what I am doing tomorrow and silently curse. What I need to do tomorrow is invite myself to his house.

The phone buzzes and my face falls as I read his answer.

I'm glad

Two words that pretty much kill the conversation. "Dammit," I whisper and look at my bedroom door. Ashlynn would know how to respond. But I don't want to ask her. My phone buzzes again with another text from Kato.

you like chess right?

Yes why?

I made something for you. can I give it to you next time I see you?

A smile plays on my lips. I try to guess what he could have made for me that relates to chess.

of course! When will that be?

I bite my lip again, waiting. He's taking longer than usual to reply. My phone finally buzzes again.

later this week there's a barn dance if you want to go with me?

I raise my eyebrows at the offer. I have never been to a dance. And later this week means I will be sitting here for days on end with just Ashlynn. With a shake of my head I answer back.

I would love to go with you Kato but maybe we can see each other before that? I could swing past your house tomorrow and pick up whatever it is you made?

> I get it, you don't want to go that long without seeing me

> Hardly

I chuckle to myself. I just can't help the happiness that spreads across my face. How is this guy always making me smile?

> I don't really want to wait that long either

> Text me your address

Of course, I have his address, but he doesn't know that.

> my dad doesn't like guests. how about we meet at the ice cream parlor again?

I let out a soft groan. I know why his dad doesn't like guests, but I need Kato to not care long enough so I can visit and check out the security. I am about to text back to convince him to meet at his house when my brother's words return to me. *We don't know that he's not.* As in, not a spy who wants to kill me. Regardless, I have to see the security system.

Then I have to go to Russia and marry a boy I have only met once.

I might never come back to Gangster Island.

> Ice cream sounds great! See you tomorrow

I set my phone down next to me. When it buzzes, I pick it up one more time.

see you then. I'll make sure to not come
down to the docks so I don't knock you into
the water again lol

Prick

That seems harsh, so I add a quick text:

lol

Kato texts back a laughing-face emoji, and I shake my
head.

———

KATO LOUNGES on the red and yellow bench outside the ice
cream parlor as if he owns the town. I catch his eye as I come
up from the gardens and cross the dirt lot toward him. I raise
my hand in greeting. "Morning!"

Kato stands, a smile forms on his face. He comes over to
me, and we meet on the sidewalk where he puts his arms
around my waist. He pulls me in and leans down, his lips
connecting with mine before I can protest.

Not that I would.

I close my eyes and reach my arms up around his neck. I
hold him tighter, pulling him closer to me. Then I remember
we are in a public place. I break away and look up into his blue
eyes. I look around to see if anyone is gawking. No one is
around this early, thank goodness.

"Hello to you, too," Kato greets.

I smile back, unable to help myself.

"I love how you do that," Kato says.

"Do what?"

"Try to pretend like you don't like me."

I raise my eyebrows. "I think you're a little full of yourself, Kato. Maybe I don't like you."

Kato gives a laugh and kisses me on the forehead before taking a step back. "I'm better at interpreting people's emotions than that. You don't want to like me for some reason, but you do. I can see it in the way you smile at me—or, rather, try not to."

I shake my head. If only he knew the truth, he wouldn't even want to look at me again. "Nah, I'm just here for the gift."

"Just a quick visit then?" Kato's expression crumples with disappointment, but he recovers fast. "I hope you don't flee this quickly from me at the dance."

The barn dance. "Of course not," I promise, though part of me doesn't want to go at all. A city of strangers watching me try to dance. Delightful. Not to mention, based on my experience at Twin Skates, a lot of girls our age will be watching us and wondering who I am and why Kato is there with me. I doubt I will have a moment to myself without eyes on me the whole evening, and I hate that. I need to lie low. Maybe I can hide in the ductwork in the barn. That is a normal place to hide, right?

Kato's eyes narrow. "You're thinking of ways to ditch me at the dance, aren't you?" he teases.

"No, of course not!" I lie. "I'm excited for the dance. I just haven't been to many dances before. Or any."

"You've never been to a dance before?" Kato says in surprise. "Really?"

"Really." There's no such thing as spy prom.

Kato grabs my hand in his and draws me flush against his body before he starts to sway back and forth.

"What are you doing?" I ask with a smile as he leads me in a dance across the sidewalk. Kato pulls me by my hands off the sidewalk and onto a patch of dirt; a historic placard states a grocery store once stood here. It's an odd, impromptu dance floor. He puts his hands on my hips, moving about in a manner that looks like dancing but isn't. "Kato—"

"Well, if you've never been to a dance before, we need to practice."

"Here in public? In an abandoned dirt lot?"

Kato tips his head. "No one cares."

"I care."

Kato lets go of my waist. He grabs one of my hands and lifts it above my head. "Aaand, spin!"

When I don't spin, he stops moving. I raise my eyebrows. "Spin?"

"Spin," he assures me, humming to a tune he must have in his head. I give in, and I twirl in the dirt, his hand guiding mine above my head. A laugh erupts from my lips as Kato embraces me again and holds my hand out in front of us. High-stepping, he tangos us in the direction our hands are pointed. At the benches, he reverses for a return stomp. When he dips me, I laugh harder—a real laugh—and I look up at his bright eyes, the outer corners crinkled with joy. With his head framed by curly hair, and the sky above, a brilliant blue behind him, he's radiant.

"I told you that you were only pretending. No one lets themselves look like a fool with someone they totally hate."

I shake my head at him. A wave of sadness passes over me, and I feel my face fall.

I don't want to do this to him.

I am glad there are a few days before the dance, so I don't have to look at him looking at me like that. I don't want to keep lying to him. Of course, I am pretending; that is my entire mission.

Kato pulls me upright, his hand warm on the small of my back. With his other hand, he brushes my hair out of my face. "You okay?" he asks, slipping his hand from my back to cup my face. He looks me in the eye, studying me, like he's never seen me before. It's like his gaze has broken through the walls of my mission. He doesn't see a persona; he just sees me.

When I'm with him, I'm not third in line. I'm not engaged. I'm not an asset in an empire. I'm just Autumn. And I feel like I can breathe.

He likes me for me. And in exchange I'm going to use him, and then leave him behind. I am going to help destroy his father, his family, and then I am going to leave. If he falls for me, if he has fallen, all I'm going to do is break his heart.

And my own.

"I have to go," I stammer, pulling away from him. I whip around and rush off for the docks.

"Autumn, wait!" Kato calls after me, but I keep my feet moving across the dirt back to the sidewalk.

This isn't right. What I am doing isn't okay. Maybe I *should* leave and let Ashlynn finish the mission.

"Autumn!" Kato grabs my arm, and I stop, turning on him sharply.

"What?" I demand, harsher than I like, my frustration striking the wrong person. Kato lets go of me. "What is it, Kato?"

"I'm sorry, I just—" Kato pulls something small from his pocket, wrapped in yellow tissue paper. "I haven't given you this yet."

I suck in a deep breath of air. Oh. I had forgotten the reason we were meeting up. My hand closes around the gift, and I take it from him. I must be the worst person alive. "Thank you," I whisper.

Kato gives me a sad look, his lips twitching upward on the right for only a moment, and I wonder if he knows what I am thinking. That I can never be my real self with him, that I am only using him because his father is after my family.

"I'll see you at the barn dance?" he asks, shoving his hands in his pockets.

I nod, my eyes still on the gift wrapped in yellow.

"Goodbye, Autumn," Kato says.

Although I don't look up, I know he has walked away.

Once I am back on the boat, seated with my back to the shore, I peel back the yellow paper, and I find a hand-carved chess piece. The queen. The most powerful piece on the board.

Over text he had said he made it himself.

My hand traces over the intricate details of the woodwork. It must have taken hours—and he gave it to me. One stray tear runs down my cheek, and I swipe it away. I start the boat to head for the island.

Rule two echoes in my head. *Don't go against the family.*

RULE 15:

TRUST YOUR INSTINCTS.

Marleen picks out my dress for me and practically squeals while doing so. She was excited when I asked her to help and keeps pointing out how she doesn't get to pick out dresses since she only has a son.

For a barn dance, her choice is a bit fancy for my taste, but Marleen waves aside my concerns. "You can never be overdressed," she argues.

"I think I can since I want to blend in and be discrete."

From the doorway outside my room, Ashlynn snorts. "Fat chance in that dress."

She's right, as much as I hate to admit it. Green velvet covers the bodice and skirt and the neck dips into a low V. The sleeves are ruffled and loose in a very modern way, not a little-kid way. The hem goes down to my knees and is loose enough to give me room to move, dance, and—as Marleen says, handing me a knife belt for my upper thigh—fight.

The blade is cool against my skin as I make my way downstairs. I didn't think Marleen would ever finish fussing. She curled my hair and added a "touch" of makeup, according to her, but the thick layer of foundation makes my nose itch. In the living room, Louie in a button-up shirt waits in a crisp collar and dress pants, and Ashlynn in a short, skin-tight blue dress with a long slit down the back.

"You look surprised," Ashlynn greets.

"I didn't realize you two were coming," I admit, taking them in.

Ashlynn rolls her eyes. "Everyone under twenty-one goes to this dance. A few parents do, too, but only to watch the younger kids. Now come on, we're going to be late. We don't want your 'date' to run off with another girl, now do we?"

Date.

That is going to take a little getting used to. At least, I hope he is still my date. I had left so abruptly the last time I saw him. Despite my remorse, only part of me hopes I haven't screwed up this mission.

When we get to the mainland, Ashlynn and Louie lead the way up to the barn. Neither have spoken since we left Gangster Island. I tried to ask about the history of Phelps, but Louie stared at me with those unsettling eyes until I looked the other way.

As much as I should like silence, I don't. I hate how they choose to say nothing. *Rule twenty: silence is golden.*

Outside the barn, the thump of music radiates through the walls. Inside, Ashlynn and Louie blend into the crowd, vanishing in opposite directions and leaving me alone at the door. As if I'm not self-conscious enough already.

The space is cavernous, its beamed ceiling soaring overhead. Clean hay covers much of the uneven and well-worn wooden floor. A faint scent of sawdust lurks beneath the smells of cheap boy cologne, even cheaper girl perfume, and body odor. Crepe-paper streamers loop from the ceiling across the length of the room, looking like they could tickle the tops of the dancers' heads. Beneath the strobing lights, a long, plastic folding table with a thin paper covering stands against the far wall. It holds a bowl of raspberry-red punch and paper cups. I wouldn't be foolish enough to drink it, of course.

My eyes scan the bobbing, weaving crowd. I didn't need Marleen to pick me out a dress at all. Several girls are in jeans and dressy tops. One I spot wears a camo sweatshirt, and jeans that tuck into what looks like cowboy boots, though she's past me before I get a good look. Even though most don gowns, I wouldn't have had to get so prettied up.

I recognize some of the students from the roller rink and others from the senior photos hanging down from light posts on Phelps' main drag. The boy who let us in at laser tag gives me a wave that I politely return as I move in and out of the crowd like a snake in tall grass.

I regret not making a better plan with Kato. I don't want to stay here long, but it is possible I could spend an hour here and never see him. Of course, I can't leave until my cousins are ready to go. We rode the pontoon over together, and as tempting as leaving them on the mainland and not seeing them again tonight is, I know I can't do that. For starters, my uncle would be awake, and he would not be amused at me ditching his kids. Second, rule two is don't go against the family, and I guess leaving them here would break that rule.

Across the room my eyes land on a familiar mop of hair. *Kato.* I make my way through the crowd toward him, careful not to interrupt anyone's dancing. I haven't bumped into this many people since my parents ditched me and Quinton in different parts of Berlin, and I had to pickpocket to get fare back to the hotel. I learned fast that the easiest way back would be to take a bus or cab, both of which required currency.

I keep an eye on Kato as he talks to his friends, keeping my hands locked behind my back as I weave around people.

Kato bends down and I lose sight of him for a moment, until his head pops back up. A little girl who couldn't be more than five sits on his shoulders, beaming at him. Even from where I am, the tinkle of her giggles float over the thrum of music. As I get closer, I can hear his voice.

"Don't pull my hair, Nadia," he requests.

"I steer you like the rat in 'Ratatouille!'" the girl calls, pleased with herself.

Kato's clear laugh fills me with warmth. I smile, too. "That would make you a rat, though, Nadia," he reminds her.

"Oh, yeah," Nadia says with displeasure. "What other movie has people being steered by the hair?"

"Is there any?" asks Seb, Kato's friend. I remember him at the roller rink. He was wearing then pretty much what he's wearing now, though a white T-shirt has replaced the muscle shirt to go with his jeans.

Kato, on the other hand, is in a dark suit jacket over a button-up shirt and no tie. Thank heavens. Had he come in jeans, with me in a fancy green velvet dress, I would have felt even more out of place.

Seb catches my eye first and offers a warm smile. "Autumn!" He waves me over.

Nadia can't help but squeal when Kato whips around. She holds on tighter, making the small clumps of Kato's hair in her fists stand up like antennas. Seeing me, Kato's face lights up. His black jacket fans away from his frame as he comes over. "Nadia, doesn't Autumn look *beautiful*?" Kato asks up to the little girl. He meets my gaze and raises one eyebrow, as if challenging me.

That clever bastard. I can't very well call him out for calling me beautiful when he says it like that. I scrunch up my nose and give a small smile as Nadia watches me.

"Which one's Autumn?" she asks with a tilt of her head so her dark curls bounce around her face.

I burst out laughing.

Kato lifts Nadia up and then lowers her to the floor. He crouches so he is at her height and curves an arm around her waist so she can't bolt off into the crowd. He points a finger up at me. "That is Autumn. She is the prettiest girl here."

"After me, of course," Nadia crosses her little arms.

"Well, of course, Nadia!" Kato says. "Don't be crazy now. She's the prettiest *after you*, and she's been foolish enough to spend her time with me since she came to Phelps."

Nadia nods. "That is rather foolish. She is pretty, though."

I crouch down, careful of my knee-length dress, and the knife strapped to my thigh. I hold my hand out to Nadia. "It's nice to meet you."

Nadia holds her small fist out in my direction. "Princesses fist bump."

"Ah, of course!" I say and bump my fist against hers.

Kato picks Nadia back up and straightens. "How about you go back with your brother for a minute?" Kato says, passing Nadia to Seb, despite his grumbles. Kato then turns back to me and offers me his elbow. "Can we talk?" he asks.

Can we talk? That never ends well. I've seen enough rom-coms and high school dramas to know that.

I force a smile on my face. "Of course." I allow him to take my arm and guide me back through the crowd. He leads me to a small side door and as he opens it, a Northwoods chill from outside strikes me. He holds the door for me, and I follow him outside.

Kato glances at me before focusing his eyeline past me. "I wanted to apologize about the other day. I clearly freaked you out. I didn't mean to. I understand if you hate me. And can't stop hating me. I don't care if it means I get to spend time with you. Anyway, I'm really sorry, and I'm glad you're here tonight."

My heart gives a flutter, surprised at his words. This is not what I expected him to say. It isn't even bad news, though I need to say something, otherwise it could be the end of whatever this is—I mean, the end of my mission. That's what is important. "Kato, you have nothing to apologize for."

Kato's eyes lock with mine again, a wrinkle of confusion pinching his brow. "You're not mad at me?"

"No!" I chuckle and take a step closer, placing a hand on

his chest. "If I was mad at you, trust me, I would let you know. I would probably be rather loud about it, too."

Kato envelopes my hand on his chest, holding me to him. "But the other day, you ran off. You were upset."

I nod my head, thinking fast. "I was sad."

"Sad?"

Sad? Really? That's what I come up with?

"Kato, I'm not going to be here that long, and I realize I kind of really like you." The words tumble out, and I realize they're the truth. "You're so different from the guys I'm around, though the guys I usually hang out with are related to me, so that's probably a good thing. Anyway, I like being around you. You see the best in me, you're fun to be around, and you don't care about what people think of you. I think that's amazing because I spend most of my time worried about how I am being perceived and...and—"

Words fail me, so I push up on my tiptoes, slip both hands around the back of Kato's head, and pull his lips to mine. A shiver runs through me that has nothing to do with the cool evening. His hands go around my waist, holding me against him. His lips are soft at first against mine. Slow and sweet. I tighten my grasp on the back of his head, my fingers tangling in his hair as I press him closer to me, kissing him deeper, faster, as if at any moment my mission could end, and he could be ripped away from me.

I pull away, looking up into his eyes. "I'm sad because I know this isn't going to be forever. It's just this summer."

Kato reaches down, tucking one of the locks Marleen spent so long curling behind my ear, a thoughtful look on his face. "Why can't it be forever? Or, at least, as long as we want? Autumn, there are so many ways to see and talk to people that you're separated from by distance. Why would we have to define when this will end?"

"Because I'm using you to gain access to your security system and then I'm going to leave and throw the burner phone you have the number for in the trash. Also, your dad is hunting my family and wants me dead." I don't actually say any of that. I bite my lip instead, look up at him and the hope in his eyes, as he looks down at me. No one has ever looked at me like this before. "You'd be okay with that?" I whisper.

Kato smiles, nodding. "Of course, I would be."

"What are we, Kato?"

Kato doesn't answer at first, and I worry I've scared him with my question. When he answers, he says, "If it's okay with you, I would like you to be my girlfriend?"

Warmth fills my insides, and I push away the guilt in my gut. "And you'd be my boyfriend? Like officially?"

"That's normally how that would work."

"I would like that a lot."

"Really?" Kato looks surprised, as if he had been expecting me to say no. Maybe his surprise makes sense because he did come into this conversation thinking I was mad at him, and that I wanted him to stay away from me.

I nod my head. "Definitely."

Kato leans down and kisses me again, his lips soft against mine, then stronger, more passionate, as the kiss deepens.

———

BACK INSIDE, I lean against the barn wall, a sense of happiness winding through me as I watch Kato dance with little Nadia, twirling her squealing form. He holds her hands as she jumps up and down and orders him around on how to spin her. He looks like he couldn't be happier than when laughing with the child.

The warmth of euphoria flushes and my nose is still cold from standing outside in Kato's arms. When we reentered the barn, Nadia had ignored Kato's hand holding mine and had dragged him onto the dance floor with her. My foggy brain didn't mind.

I have a boyfriend.

A *boyfriend*.

Kato likes me.

I shot the guy with a paintball, and he still likes me.

I know I have no reason to be so happy. What I am doing isn't fair to Kato. And no matter what he thinks, as soon as I leave, I know I will never see him again, as much as I want to.

As I watch him on the dance floor, I realize that if I don't go to his house, I can stay here. The mission continues. Perhaps I could get stationed here, and Kato's hope won't be misplaced.

"You like him," Ashlynn's voice cuts through my happy fog.

"What?" I look over at her. I didn't sense her approach me. She has so much more skill at these things than I do. And she read me. "Who?" I ask, though we both know who. I have been ogling him since we came back in.

"Oh, my God, you've fallen for your target!" Ashlynn whisper-screams. "Do you realize how messed up that is? You're playing that poor sap on the floor. What do you think he's going to do when he figures out you're not some sweet rich girl?"

"I have not fallen for Kato!" I say through gritted teeth. "Shut up!"

"You think he's still going to like you when he realizes why you're really in Phelps?"

I look back at the dance floor. Ashlynn has popped my happy balloon, and I know she is right. You can't build anything on lies. From a family of secrets, crime, and deception, Ashlynn and I know that better than anyone.

Besides, I am still engaged. And the mission must be completed if I want to save my family.

"What are you ladies talking about?" Seb asks from my other side, and I cover my guilt and concern with a smile.

Ashlynn leans past me toward Seb. "Autumn and Kato are

officially dating," she says with a grin as if it's normal gossip. "And she really likes him."

Seb gives me a playful punch on the shoulder. "Congrats!"

"Thank you both," I say, staring off past the happy people dancing. Kato and Nadia are no longer on the dance floor.

"Well, if Kato wouldn't mind sharing you for one dance, do you mind if I steal you away from Mary?"

Who's Mary? I wonder, as Seb holds out his hand for me to take. Then I remember, that's the name folks know Ashlynn as in Phelps. Because, unlike me, who was assigned this for one summer, her entire life has been one mission.

I can't imagine never being myself. I've spent little time here, and I couldn't even keep my name a secret. She's kept her whole life a secret. Growing up, when I heard that she went to public school, I was a little jealous. She got to make real memories and have friends who aren't knowledgeable about the best type of poison to use for a death to look like a stroke. But being here, being a part of the world she has to occupy as Mary, I realize Ashlynn must be so lonely. Not enough training to fit into our world, but too much to fit into theirs.

"She's been practically begging to get away from me," Ashlynn teases, her voice syrupy sweet, and her smile a little too friendly. It is weird—it's not the Ashlynn I know. "Go on, baby bird! Have some fun."

"Please, get me away from her," I tease back, and Seb laughs as I take his hand and he leads me onto the dance floor, once again out of ear shot of my cousin.

Seb smiles at me as we dance, we don't even touch. We could fit another person between us, but I'm glad he's as awkward as I feel. "I wanted to ask you about Mary," Seb says. "You two are pretty close, yeah?"

I nod my head. "Practically family."

"Do you think... I'm thinking about asking her out, like on a date. Like a real date, just me and her. Do you think she would say yes?"

I glance back to where we had left Ashlynn alone. If Seb knew her—not as Mary—would he still like her? He had fallen for a fake her, just like Kato had fallen for me. But fake or not, my happiness tonight was real. And I wished that sort of joy for my cousin as well. I turn back to Seb. "I can't say for sure, but I think you should ask her."

"Yeah?" Seb grins. "I'm going to, then."

"Going to what?" a voice says from behind me. I look back to find Kato staring at Seb, but not in his usual friendly way. Kato's hand wraps around my waist and holds me from behind. "What are you two up to?"

"I was just asking Autumn what she sees in you," Seb teases. I giggle, but Kato remains pressed against my back, not laughing at all at the joke, his arm around me tightening.

"That's not funny, Seb," Kato says.

I turn and look back at Kato, and he loosens his grasp. "I was just filling Seb in on how you and I are dating now," I say.

The tension in Kato's shoulders release and he lets me go, returning his hand to his side. "Cool."

"Where's Nadia?" Seb asks.

"I left her with Mary," Kato says. His grin returns once more, though it's not as warm as it was when I had first arrived.

"That I have to see."

Kato's hand entwines with mine as he leads me off the dance floor, Seb right behind us. He guides me over to where Ashlynn crouches down on the floor against a wall, tying Nadia's shoe. Nadia is tying knots into Ashlynn's hair at the same time. I laugh, and Ashlynn looks up. "Help me," she mouths, and Seb is by her side, pulling his sister away.

Kato wraps his arm around my shoulders.

The rest of the night is tame. Kato and I dance a few times. Nadia falls asleep in Seb's arms. The knife under my dress stays hidden.

Around midnight the petite woman who owns the barn

turns off the music and turns up the lights to give everyone the message that it's time to go home. Kato guides me through the crowd out into the night air.

"Can I take you home?" he asks as we stand outside the barn, the last sounds of the dance dissipating as people leave.

I wrap my arms around myself, to shield the cold as we stand like a rock in a river with streams of people rushing past us on either side. None of those people are Ashlynn or Louie. "I can't," I say, despite wanting him to drive me home, drop me off at the door, and have a movie moment kiss on the front stoop. "I live on the island, remember? Not really easy to just drop me off." But I don't want to leave and go back to my uncle's house. For the first time ever, I have a boyfriend.

The girl who's in line to take over an empire, and engaged to someone else, has a boyfriend.

"You know, my dad owns a boat. This is a lake town. Most people own some sort of boat. Or raft. Have you ever ridden a canoe in a dress?"

I laugh, but I know I have to turn him down. "Sorry, Kato."

"Hey are you cold?"

"Freezing." *Where is Ashlynn and Louie?*

Kato slides off his suit jacket and places it around me. It's warm, and I slide my hands through the sleeves.

"But you'll be cold," I try to protest. He shakes his head. "Thank you," I say.

"What are boyfriends for?"

I have no idea. I've never had one before.

"Wearing his jacket?" Ashlynn whistles from behind me. "You two must be getting serious."

Despite the cold, my face flushes.

"She is my girlfriend now," Kato says.

Girlfriend. Me.

Ashlynn stands with Seb as Louie waits about five feet behind them. Nadia is asleep in Seb's arms. Her head flops over one of his arms, and her hair, along with a bead of drool ooze down toward the dirt.

"Autumn, are you ready to go?" Ashlynn asks.

"You know, I could bring her home," Kato offers. I turn to look at him. Hadn't I just told him no? Why is he asking my cousin? An uneasy pit rocks in my gut.

"Only if you want my dad to point his hunting rifle at you." Ashlynn holds out a hand to me like I'm a small child. With her palm open, she reaches for mine to take hers. I can't tell if it's friendly, or demeaning. "Come on. I don't want to be out too late."

"If you two keep Mary from getting home, she's going to be a grump tomorrow, and no one wants that." Seb teases.

Kato's face falls. "I don't think this concerns you, Seb. How about you say goodnight to Mary, and I'll meet you soon?"

Seb put his hands up in a surrender pose as best he can without dropping Nadia. "Take your time." He turns to Ashlynn. "Goodnight Mary," he says before nodding to me and slipping into the crowd of people headed for their homes.

"We should be going to," Ashlynn presses.

"You're sure I can't bring you safely home? It seems like the gentlemanly thing to do. It's dark out," Kato reasons.

I shake my head and kiss him on the cheek. "Goodnight, boyfriend. I'll see you tomorrow."

He doesn't appear happy, but I don't give him time to protest as I take Ashlynn's hand and we slip into the night. "He was acting weird, right?" I whisper to her.

"A little pushy," Ashlynn agrees, letting go of my hand as soon as Kato can't see us. The switch flips and she's no longer Mary.

He seemed more than a little pushy. Maybe I'm reading too much into it, but he's acting the way I have since trying to gain access to his house. Even after a perfect night, I still can't assess how much he knows.

AUTUMN

AGE 10

"It said it was breathable mesh," I muttered as Nellie, one of the house staff, pulled the corset strings up my back tighter. I held my hands outward, like a stiff doll, not sure what else to do with them.

"I think it looks beautiful, Miss. You are going to be the prettiest ten-year-old," Nellie said, tying off the strings. "There."

"Do I have to wear all this?" I put my arms down, looking at myself in my bedroom mirror. The sleeves puffed out, and like the rest of the tight gold fabric, they sparkled beneath my bedroom's small chandelier.

"Yes, Miss."

"I don't like it."

Nellie shook her head, our eyes meeting in the mirror. "That's not true and you know it. I need to go make sure everyone else is ready. Quinton is escorting you downstairs. There you will meet your father. I can trust you not to be late, right?"

"Yeah," I assured.

Nellie said something I didn't hear as she left, and I sank into a glittery gold pool of fabric on the floor.

My parents had organized a ball-like event to greet the Al-amin family to the United States. The minor families of the Bancrofts, Varons, Savinos, Kodas, and Rosingols had all sent representatives. I *however was supposed to come down and be put on display—a pretty porcelain doll they could look at and not touch. Quinton would get to meet and socialize with everyone, whereas my mother had bought me a dress so poofy I wouldn't be able to get close to anyone if I tried.*

My father's voice echoed from the hall, blending into the music playing downstairs. With a huff of air, I got myself back on my feet. If I went downstairs long enough to be presented and grab a plate of food, I could slip back up here without anyone noticing.

I grabbed a necklace off my dresser and strung it around my neck as I made my way over to my door but stopped when I heard my uncle, and then my father's short response. They were arguing.

I pressed my ear to the cool wood of my door, the necklace forgotten in my hand. I could make out their voices.

"It doesn't look right that you always leave them behind," my father snipped.

"They are my children, Michael, not yours. It is my choice to make."

Very few people were allowed to address my father by his first name. Unless the person is of high rank, they were supposed to call him Mr. Alderidge. Close family and friends held the exception to the rule. I pressed my ear harder, listening closer.

"What are you so afraid of here? Ashlynn is not her mother; she's not going to run off wi—"

"Stop!" my uncle's voice boomed. "They are my children, and when I say they are not coming to an event, they are not coming. They will be well trained, and ready when they join this world. But I get to decide when that is—not you."

"We had already joined when we were their age."

"She is a child. Louie is a child. They're all children. This game we play, it's not right for children to be a part of."

"If we don't trust the children, we will lose everything," my father reminded.

"Just because you're ready to marry off your ten-year-old, doesn't mean I am."

I looked down—they were talking about me.

I didn't fully understand then, but I had known a lot of kids from all the families would be in attendance. I couldn't then imagine why my uncle would be so upset with his kids coming too.

My father paused before continuing. "I respect whatever you decide for your children. I just would hate for them to miss this because of your fears."

"Our father would roll over in his grave if he saw the way you are raising your children," Uncle sneered.

I pulled away from the wooden door. I no longer wanted to hear the rest of the argument.

RULE 16:

ALWAYS HAVE A WAY OUT.

"Absolutely not," Uncle replies as we walk together through the forested island. He knows the way around, and his feet are sure, whereas I have to keep looking down, watching for animal droppings, loose twigs, muddy patches, and anything else unexpected that might trip me up.

"How is he supposed to trust me if I don't appear to trust him?" I demand, tailing after.

"I think you've forgotten who his family is."

"I haven't!" I insist. "I'm just suggesting one family game night."

"We don't have family game night," my uncle reminds me.

"I know that, but Kato doesn't. If he comes to our house, then there's a better chance he will return the gesture and invite me over to his."

"Was this your idea or his?"

"Mine!" If it was Kato's, I wouldn't have brought it to my uncle. This would reveal why he insists on seeing the island. If there is a why. I hope there isn't a why. "I came up with it."

"Ashlynn thinks you're getting a little too close."

I steady my balance on a hunk of moss. A mosquito buzzes

in my ear. "I'm convincing at my job," I reply, trying to wave off Ashlynn's accusation—that I'm falling for my target. That isn't why I want to invite Kato over.

"She also says they know you as Autumn in Phelps."

"That is my name."

"Rule three."

"I know, never use your real name on a mission," I recite to him. "But when I first met Kato, he knocked me off a dock and I was wet and angry, and I slipped up. It won't happen again."

Uncle stops walking, and I nearly run into his backside. With a quick sidestep, I move next to him. "He knocked you off the dock?" My uncle looks upset.

"Well, kind of. He startled me, and I slipped on the dock. I don't have a lot of experience being on docks. And I fell backward into the water. And I was fine."

Uncle closes his eyes. "I told my brother this was a bad idea."

"What?" His only brother is my father.

"You are third in line for this family, you do realize that, yes, Autumn?"

The fact that my father, mother, and Quinton would have to die for that to happen races through my mind. "Yes, Uncle. What does that have to do with this?"

"What would have happened if you had hit your head on the dock and died?"

"What?" I look at him in confusion. "I guess then you would be third in line?"

My uncle shakes his head. "Your father thinks it's wise to send you and your brother on these dangerous missions, as if you kids are invincible. But you're not. What you are is the collective head of a powerful family that is crumbling."

I cross my arms. "Like you and my father never trained, never went on missions when you were younger. What you're saying is hypocritical."

Uncle's face twists and I know I'm out of line. Uncle is my superior while I'm here. I need to be careful, or else I could find myself on a plane to Russia before the end of the day.

"Sorry," I say. "I just... I am..."

"No," my uncle says. "When your father and I were younger, we were not being hunted like you are now. How many bases worldwide does our family have?"

I think back to my father's history lesson. "Eighty-seven belong solely to the Alderidge family. There are roughly one-hundred-and-thirty-four more places belonging to minor families who have sworn allegiance to us that would welcome any member of our family with open arms at any time. The number of these bases are growing every day, though."

"You learned your lessons well. Your memorization is excellent. But we are down to twenty-one bases that belong to us. The minor families have all closed their doors, except for those hoping to overthrow us while we are weakened. They have seen us falling, and they have wisely turned on us. In less than a month, we have lost sixty-six bases. So no, I will not welcome with open arms the man whose father is responsible for it all. He is not welcome on Gangster Island, and if he so much as ever steps foot here, I will kidnap him and use him as a hostage against his father. Do I make myself clear, Autumn? That boy is not welcome here."

I nod my head, as his words sink in. When my uncle walks away, I don't follow him. As soon as I am sure he can't see me anymore, I slump against a tree trunk and sit down on the cool ground, my heart racing. I knew it was bad, everyone had said as much, but we've lost all of our allies and three-fourths of our people? I had no idea. We aren't in bad shape—we are screwed.

No wonder Quinton must marry Naomi. No wonder my parents insisted I marry Dimitri. We don't have much of a choice if we want to survive. I know the way my mother thinks; our quick marriages are her idea. She comes from a minor family. She knows survival isn't always pretty, but if her children are integrated at the tops of other major families, then we at least are safer. It wouldn't be about saving the Alderidges for her, it would be about saving her children. We have to marry quick, before the major families no longer deem us worth marrying.

A raspy breath escapes my lips, and tears roll down my cheeks. I raise my sleeve to my eyes, wiping them dry. I need to succeed on my mission; otherwise, I risk losing my family. I need to betray Kato. I need to stop letting my heart get involved. I am an Alderidge, and it is damn well time I start behaving like one.

My phone buzzes in my pocket, and I pull it out. I have a text from Kato.

> you busy?

Besides dealing with an existential crisis, no, not at all. All's peachy.

> Could we do something tomorrow?

Kato texts back just as fast. It's as if he is waiting for my response and nothing matters more to him. I swallow back the lump in my throat as I read his response.

> sure! I have a fun idea. pick you up at the usual dock?

> If you don't push me in first lol

> lmao! Well I'll always be there to jump in and save you if you trip and fall again ☺ see you tomorrow

> see you then.

I shove my phone back into my pocket. Part of me thinks I should leave for Russia tonight and let Ashlynn take over. I don't know how I'll be able to face Kato tomorrow.

RULE 17:

CHAOS IS YOUR FRIEND.

Hours later, I'm still sitting on the forest floor, my back against a tree, bark getting in my hair. I don't know what to do. I only have one choice, and I don't like it.

I have to choose my family over a boy I just met, no matter how sweet, how handsome, how funny he is. No matter how much he likes me. It doesn't matter. Kato can't matter.

Through the trees, I watch the sun set; purples and pinks bounce off puffs of clouds, with golden streaks, all of it reflecting on the glassy lake. Down the shoreline, Dublin's Pub starts up its movie night. Marleen had invited me to go when we were getting ready for the barn dance. I had politely declined, not because I didn't want to be trapped on a little boat bobbing in the water in front of an inflatable screen with her and her son while watching an animated movie, but because of my mission. I must remind myself why I'm here. And it's not to hang out with Marleen and her son.

As darkness settles on the island, the mosquitoes wake up. The dragonflies have gone to bed and aren't around to feast on the flying bloodsuckers anymore. I swat at them, leaving smears of blood and skeeter guts on my hand, my pant leg, and anywhere there's exposed flesh. When one lands on my face, I decide it's time to go in.

I shove off the tree, using it to stand, as I get to my feet in the semidarkness. I pull my phone out of my pocket and turn on its flashlight, an instant beacon for the angry swarms. I walk quickly, careful not to trip.

The glow from the house lights the walkway, and I flick off my phone flashlight. One thing I won't miss about this place: the awful bugs. They're everywhere. Skeeters. Biting black flies. Those tiny biters—noseeums. Even inside, mosquitoes sometimes buzz in your ear as you fall asleep, and small gnats can get through window and door screens to cloud around lamps and other lights. Lighted windows needed to be closed so the glow didn't attract anything you didn't want crawling on you while you slept. Uncle recommended drawing the curtains as well.

My hand finds the screen door handle when I hear the first shot. It rings out into the clear night. Instinctively, I move to the side of the door and crouch down, pressing my back against the building. A bush blocks my view of the shoreline as I search for the source of the sound.

Another shot rings out, but I don't hear any people. Or screaming. Nothing except the buzz of mosquitoes.

I pull my phone out and text Ashlynn.

> What is going on???

After a moment, my phone buzzes with a reply.

> What do you mean? Where are you?

> I'm outside. I hear shots fired. You okay??

> OMG LMAO!!

I look at my phone confused.

What?

Those are fireworks moron

Another bang rings out, and this time I hear the echo after the sound. I move a few feet away from the house, glancing toward Phelps. A sparkle of purple fades out in the air. Fireworks. Not gunfire. I pinch my eyes shut in embarrassment, shaking my head. I am too on edge. My phone buzzes in my hand again, and I look down—it's another message from Ashlynn.

They're coming from Phelps if you don't believe me look that way

I believe you.

I shove my phone back into my pocket and head inside, wishing my brother was here. He would laugh at me, sure, but he would also make me feel better and listen to me vent about my mission. Will he still do that when he is married? Reality cracks through the status quo I have known my whole life. No, he will move out and get his own place. It hadn't dawned on me that we would never live under the same roof again. I'm filled with boiling anger.

This isn't fair. None of this is fair. We probably won't even be together next Christmas. Quinton will be with his new family.

I kick my boots off, leaving them by the door, as I enter the dark house.

"Autumn?" I jump in surprise at my uncle's voice. He sits on the couch as if waiting for me. "I just received word from your parents."

The solemn tone in his voice makes my stomach drop. I

grab the door handle for support—or so I can bolt, depending on what he has to report. "Are they okay?"

"The base they were staying at took heavy fire."

"Oh God."

"We lost another base, and your mother suffered minor injuries, but they're alive. They got out," my uncle assures me.

I take a breath, let go of the door, and walk to my uncle, sitting in a chair next to him. "What did they have to say then? Am I being pulled?" If things are as bad as my uncle said, the sooner we can cement the Russians' help the better.

He shakes his head. His jaw juts out more than it usually does, tense, set. I brace for the news. I could be married by morning. I might never see Kato again.

"No," Uncle says. With one word, I feel like I can breathe. I am also confused. We are in so much danger. The correct course of action to me would be my going to Russia. But I'm not going to argue for that. "Your father wanted to offer you an incentive to complete your mission quicker." The tone in my uncle's voice says he doesn't agree. I assume that he thinks I'd be safer if I left, not safer if I try to speed through a dangerous assignment.

"An incentive?" The last time my father proposed an incentive, I got a Kit Kittredge American Girl doll, the one known for snooping for her newspaper during the Great Depression. I am a little harder to bribe these days.

"He tells me you want to work in Paris?"

That's my dream gig if we survive this: No active missions, no being chased or shot at, no cute targets to fall in love with, just studying people and supporting others' missions. "He's going to station me in Paris once I finish my mission here?" I allow hope to enter my voice, even though Quinton made it clear that once I was done, I would be going to Russia to get married.

My uncle watches me with that same unsettling look Louie

always has on his face. "He said you could choose anywhere you wanted. You could have your choice of base."

"My choice?" The question tumbles from my lips. The person being stationed never gets to choose. One look at my uncle's expression confirms his opposing views on nepotism. I don't think the weight of my parents and Quinton's near demise on my uncle's conscience helps the situation.

On occasion my father will listen to requests for where someone would like to be stationed and give in, but family members never get to pick. Uncle didn't pick Gangster Island.

My uncle nods. "Unprecedented, I know. But he needs you to wrap this up quickly; otherwise, the deal goes away."

I nod, my thoughts racing. This deal should never exist in the first place. I should execute a mission with precision, not speed—I need to think on this. "Goodnight, Uncle," I say and hurry upstairs to my room.

If I can choose anywhere, I could choose to stay here with Kato and not be a terrible person for leading him on. If he could be understanding of what I had to do next, and I could tell him after my mission is complete why I did what I'm going to do, maybe we could date, for real, without it being a mission or fake. Perhaps we could be a real couple.

A knock on my door startles me from my thoughts, and I hurry over. Every door in my uncle's house has a peephole so you can look out into the hallway—it's for security. I'm glad they are there because Ashlynn stands on the other side of the door.

"I'm going to bed!" I call through the knotty pine.

"Open up, Gunfire," she responds.

I much prefer being called Gunfire to Princess, but neither nickname is from a place of kindness. Nonetheless, I open the door, and she charges into my room, turning to face me at the foot of my bed.

"What?" I ask, watching her. "What is it?" I softly close the door behind us.

Ashlynn shakes her head, her soft curls bouncing as she leans against my bed, her manicured nails digging into the soft comforter. "You don't know much about this place, do you?"

I sigh as I look at my window and away from my cousin. "I'm sorry that I thought the fireworks were gunfire. Honest mistake, sheesh. It won't happen again."

"I'm not talking about that."

I turn back to her. "What are you talking about then?"

"All information can be useful, right? Vy is missing. While you may have just arrived here in Wisconsin, I've been playing this scene for a while. Seb likes me, so ask and I shall receive. And what I have received this time is concerning. Apparently, no one has seen her since you and her talked at the doors to the roller rink."

"I didn't do anything to her."

"Of course not."

"Then what is this?"

Ashlynn stands up straight. "It's called sharing information, cousin. I know everyone around here thinks Kato is this sweet innocent thing, but I'm the one who has known him for years. It was the right call, giving the mission to you, because he doesn't like me much. But he doesn't like me much because I can see through his façade. Vy was new last year. She came in around the same time the whispers started about the fifth family. I think Kato's father hired her as security."

"Karen White."

"What?"

"Her real name is Karen White. She was on the short list to marry Quinton but didn't get an invite."

Ashlynn nods. "Well, she's missing now. I contacted Aunt Magdalena. So far, nothing. I don't think Kato is as innocent as you want to believe, and I do think you need to be more careful. He can be... possessive."

I want to dismiss my cousin, to shove her out the door and slam it shut, but I can't help but think back to the barn dance.

How Kato acted when Seb and I were dancing, how tightly he had held me to him. It had made me pause then and makes me pause now. I don't know Kato as well as I would like to. "Explain."

Ashlynn moves over and pats me on the shoulder. "He was never interesting, nothing noteworthy, just an average American teen until recently. But by what Seb told me, his last girlfriend didn't decide to go to boarding school in Maine to get away from her parents. She did it to get away from him."

I stand there, dumbfounded as she moves past and leaves my room, closing my door behind her. So much more than Kato being a bad guy could have led to a rough breakup, but I still find myself a little shaken as I go to bed.

AUTUMN

AGE 16

"I don't like him," I said again, my nose still cold from the outdoors as I pulled Dimitri's bomber hat off my head.

"Who?" my father asked, joining my mother and me in our home's entryway under the glow of an outdated chandelier.

"The man who came to America," I said, mocking Dimitri's Russian accent. "'I am Dimitri Daxterov and no woman of mine vill be fixing the gate box. I vill send you men and vodka and a parka because you are cold'."

"Autumn, you barely know the boy; this is hardly fair," my mother countered.

My father looked between me and my mother in confusion. "I'm sorry, when exactly did Autumn meet Dimitri? Their first meeting is still being planned between Dimitri's father and me. The Daxterovs are not going to be happy to learn you've already met."

"They're going to be even more unhappy when they learn I'm not marrying him," I said, crossing my arms and giving my father a cold stare. His face twisted in anger.

"That's enough, Autumn," my mother said.

My father's voice wavered as he struggled to remain composed. "No, if she doesn't want to marry him, she shouldn't have to. But Autumn, you should at least meet him first. Properly."

"I did meet him properly," I argued. "Just now, outside. Mother sent me out to see about the gate, which was fine, so me and Dimitri could 'happen' to bump into each other. There was nothing there. No spark. No magic."

"You don't know if you like someone based on a brief conversation," my mother said.

"No, but you can easily decide if you don't like someone based on a brief conversation. So, you can call off the engagement."

"No, I can't," Father said, his face flushed but his composure still maintained.

I looked at him in surprise. "You always said that if I didn't like the guy, I wouldn't have to marry him."

My father nodded his head. "And you don't. But you have to meet him first and go on one date. If I call off the engagement after he visits for no reason, it would be a declaration of war, which we can't afford. The Daxterovs will understand if you two have properly met, but standing outside in the frigid cold looking at a gate doesn't count. Engagements aren't that easily broken."

"But—"

"Your father has made up his mind," my mother snapped. "Enough of this, Autumn."

"So, what am I supposed to do? Just pretend I like him?"

"Did he say anything derogatory to you? Did he hurt or touch you?" my father asked.

I hid the bomber hat behind my back. "No. He was a perfect gentleman. True 1800s charm. Offered to send us a 'man' to watch the gate, so I would never have to go out in the snow again. Though if you both are shipping me off to Russia, I don't think I'll be able to avoid snow."

"No one is shipping you anywhere," my mother said.

My father nodded. "You have to give him a shot. At the very least. For the family's sake. Love isn't built in five minutes."

RULE 18:

IF YOU MESS UP, FESS UP.

"Rock climbing?" I guess.

"Nope!" Kato says as he drives the truck, a smile on his face. "Guess again."

I ride shotgun, trying to figure out where we are going, and do my best to ignore my mother's voice screaming in my head for getting in a vehicle without knowing. "Are we—going back to the Piggly Wiggly?"

"The Pig is the other direction," Kato reminds me.

"Right, right. We're walking through downtown Eagle River?" I ask, "checking out the tourist-trap T-shirt and fudge shops."

Kato shakes his head. "It's colder than rock climbing, but warmer than going to the moon."

I make a few more guesses but end up laughing at my ridiculous theories, and soon Kato is laughing, too. "Okay, then where are we going?" I giggle. "Come on, you can't keep me in the dark forever. I have a right to know."

"Is that right?"

"That is right." We have been driving for about an hour, heading south on a two-lane highway. As much as I trust Kato,

I remind myself this is still a mission, and we don't know how involved he is in his father's operations. According to standard practice, I had sent my location on my cell phone to Marleen so someone could monitor my destination. Not that I think Kato will do anything to hurt me.

"Okay, fine," Kato finally relents. "I was hoping to wait until we were another hour down the road, but we're going to Devil's Lake."

"Another hour? How far away is this devil?"

"Don't be mad. It's like three and a half hours away."

My eyes go wide as I look at him. "Three and a half hours? Kato—"

"Hey, I asked if you were busy today, you said no, sooo..."

A laugh spills from my lips. "So, you took that to mean we should go drive for seven hours to see a lake? You do realize we were on a lake, right? You picked me up at a lake. And we just passed a sign for another lake. There are lakes everywhere here."

"Hey, laugh all you want, but those lakes don't have cliffs you can jump off of into the water."

"Wait, what?" the smile on my face fades. "We're jumping off a cliff?"

"Only the best cliff for my girlfriend," he says with pride.

My stomach flip flops as he calls me that again. It gives me butterflies. I swallow down both the flutter in my stomach and my fear of heights, and I force a smile. "That sounds great, Kato."

"You're not excited," Kato notes, and I silently swear at myself for not being better at hiding my emotions. "I'm sorry, this was kind of a big step, I should have asked first instead of just planning. We can turn back if you want, stop at some small diner, have a date like normal people do."

"Normal people? Are you saying we're not normal?" I ask with a teasing voice. I know I sure as hell am not normal, but he is. I think.

"Of course not. You know what I mean. Most people don't go cliff-jumping on their first date as boyfriend and girlfriend."

"I also don't like most people."

Kato nods. "That's true. You barely like me."

"Shut up, that's not true." I give a playful punch to his arm that isn't on the steering wheel, and he starts to laugh, which makes me grin. "I like you."

"I like you, too," he says, mirroring my expression.

For years I've wondered where Dimitri might take me for a first date. Certainly not a place with "Devil" in the name to jump off a cliff. I imagine Dimitri in a wool overcoat, hurdling off a cliff and yelling "Ameriiiiiiicaaaaa!" while he plummets through the air and splashes in the cold water below, and I can't help but laugh to myself.

Kato and I talk most of the way about movies (his favorite Christmas movie is *Gremlins*), the weather (it's nice in Phelps in the summer but snowy in the winter; perfect for snowmobiling, which he insists I will be doing with him), favorite animals (pigs for me, though I chose the first animal I thought of), school (he once got in trouble for finger-painting the cover of his mother's romance book), and what we like to do for fun.

I censor the stories I share so I don't reveal anything about my family, but it's nice to share, and Kato is easy to talk to. Ashlynn's concerns from the night before fade from my thoughts. They no longer seem to be a problem, and instead, have become irrelevant to my mission.

We pass another sign for Devil's Lake. I've been enjoying my conversations with Kato so much that I am sad we're near our destination. Kato focuses on catching the right exit. He pulls the truck into an empty dirt lot and parks facing a drop-off to the lake below.

"Whoa, the water's really far down," I comment, looking out the windshield as Kato turns the car off.

Kato flashes me a grin. "What? Are you scared? Are you going to bail on me?"

Tension sets in my jaw. I know it doesn't matter if we jump or not. I am still on a date with Kato, and he won't be mad if I do bail on him. But something about the tone of his voice when he asks if I'm scared makes me want to prove him wrong.

"I'm not bailing," I promise. "Though I wish you would have told me we were coming here so I could have worn a swimsuit," I add, putting my phone in his truck's glove box. No way I'm bringing it in the water with me.

Kato laughs. "I was worried you would come up with something more fun for us to do."

"More fun than possibly jumping to our deaths? And what would be wrong with that?" I ask as we both unbuckle and get out of the car. Kato locks it up behind him and shoves his keys into his pocket. He waits for me in front of the vehicle, his hand outstretched for me to take, which I do with a smile.

"You'd pick something closer to home, and I like driving. It's nice to just sit and talk. If we hadn't done that, we wouldn't have had our discussion on who would win a fight: one hungry, angry, but also bloodied gremlin or one large, ravenous pig."

"The pig would win," I say again. Kato guides me from the gravel parking area toward the cliffs with skilled feet that indicate he's been here before.

"A pig cannot beat a gremlin!" Kato argues and then laughs. "Please, let's not start this again."

"Hey, you're the one who brought it up." I give him a playful nudge. His keys rattle, and I risk a glance at his pocket. I note that his keys are hanging halfway out. If I can get his house key, I can give that to my uncle, and maybe I won't have to reveal who I am. With a key, the home security shouldn't be much of a concern, right?

"Is something wrong?" Kato asks, stopping at the edge of

one of the cliffs. His hair is the same color as the ocean-drenched sand in the midday sun. I look over the edge, but I can't see the beach below us, just the cliffside plunging into choppy waves.

The thought of stealing his keys evaporates into the sunlight sparkling in his eyes. "No, I'm just worried you're going to lose your keys in the water and then we'll be stuck here forever." I am close, after all, to finishing this mission, not that I want it to end anytime soon.

Kato looks down at his pocket and chuckles. "Good catch," he says as he pulls his keys out and grips them in one hand, his other hand firmly holding mine as he walks to the edge of the cliff. "You ready now?"

I look down at the water below. So far below. "You have done this before, right?"

"Once," Kato says with a shrug.

"And it went, okay?"

"No, Autumn, two of my friends were killed, and so I thought this would make a perfect date."

For a moment I can't tell if he's serious, or sarcastic. Maybe he brought me here to shove me off a cliff and kill me. We're far enough away he would have a head start in getting rid of my body. Maybe Ashlynn was right.

"I'm kidding." Kato sighs. "Everything went fine. It's really fun. Trust me."

I look down at the water, bright blue and churned up. The cliff isn't high enough where my dad would yell at me for doing this, but it *is* high enough to receive my mother's admonishments. Of course, my mother isn't here. No one is here but me and Kato.

In Phelps, a safety net is always in place; one of my family's men—or Ashlynn or Abby—could be watching me, waiting for me to mess up so they can sweep in. But here I am truly alone, on a solo mission with a cute boy. And I don't have my phone to call for help if things go south. This is literally going to be a leap of faith.

I look at Kato, and all my concerns fade away. None of it matters. What matters is right in front of me. "Ready," I say. And we jump.

AUTUMN

AGE 10

"Don't stay still!" my father barked from the pool's edge as Quinton lunged at me again, grabbing me from behind in a headlock and forcing me underwater. He kept his hold on me light. We were supposed to be training, but Quinton never trained properly against me. It didn't help to know how to flip a seventy-pound, ten-year-old girl if you planned to square off against two-hundred-plus-pound men with muscles.

I flailed underwater until I got my foot to the bottom of the pool and used it to curl into the fetal position. With Quinton's arms locked around me from behind, my curled position hindered his ability to control his body and allowed me to spin him off me.

I preferred fighting underwater to on land. There were fewer hard landings, and I could do cooler spins in the water. Though I wished my father would let me have my hair down during training so it could swirl around me like the mermaids in the movies. Father was insistent, thanks to my mother: All hair must be pulled back tightly.

Quinton lunged at my midsection, knocking me back. We seemed to move in slow motion. I kicked up at him and hit him square in the gut, causing him to release me.

Quinton pushed to the surface. He broke out of the water and continued to tread.

Looking up through the churning foam, I could see Quinton's mouth moving. He was saying something to Father. As I got closer to the surface, I could see Father was ignoring him. His eyes instead were glued on me. When I came out of the water, he nodded his head at me before looking to my brother.

I lunged up at Quinton, grabbing him around the thighs and pulling him back under. My father blew his whistle, but not before Quinton sucked in a mouthful of pool water in surprise. I let go of him and returned to the surface, feeling proud, feeling big-time. Quinton came to the surface, too, coughing water and glaring at me. His face was bright red, matching the locks of wet hair he pushed from his face.

"Good job, Autumn," my father said. "Quinton, that was disappointing."

I gave Quinton one triumphant nod before swimming to the pool's edge and boosting myself up and out of the water.

"That's not fair!" Quinton exploded. "We were training her today, not me! She wasn't supposed to attack me!"

My father shook his head. "You must always be aware of your surroundings. Be ready. If Autumn was a threat you thought you had neutralized, and she did that, she could have taken you out. She could have killed you. You need to be prepared for an assault at any time."

RULE 19:

CONFIDENCE IS KEY.

The water rushes toward me. Whitecaps swell below my feet. I have jumped from higher before but with a harness on to ease my way down. Still, I don't scream. Next to me, Kato yells with delight and pure joy as the sound of the wind rushes past my head and ears.

When we hit the water, I lose Kato's hand. My body plunges down into the murky blue. This time, I get my mouth closed, unlike at the dock in Phelps when I fell in and swallowed a mouthful of lake that I had to cough back out. I press my lips together even though I want to scream at the shock of cold when the lake envelops me.

My feet don't find the bottom in the chilly waters, which is probably a good thing. Shallow water could be deadly. I kick upward, propelling myself to the surface, and I break through with a gasp, my hair wet and matted over my face. With a "WHOOP!", I push the hair up over my head and search the surface of the sun-shimmered water for Kato. A warm breeze helps ease the chill. "Oh man, that was awesome!" I don't see him, though. He isn't back on the surface. "Kato?"

I yell for him again, fear seizing my gut. I splash my face

into the water. I need to find him. The fear twists. The water is too murky and occupied by fish and weeds. I don't see him anywhere. I take in a deep breath and dive down, looking for Kato, feeling for him as the water stings my eyes. It's like he vanished.

I bob back to the surface, gasping in air. Still no sign of him.

Someone grabs me from behind, and my instincts and lifetime of training take over. Shut off emotions, those get in the way. Adrenaline fills my brain. Steady your breathing—you can't help anyone if you panic. I know what to do. And if I'm wrong, I could die. I pitch forward, my head going underwater, and I spin whoever it is behind me over my shoulder into the water. We do a complete flip, and I push the person into the depths.

I break free. They're off me.

Now I need to be faster so I can get away from my attacker. I start to swim frantically toward the shore's rock face. It's not far. If the person is stunned, I may be able to get there before they even recover. Then it's just a foot race.

Glancing back, though, I see who it is. And I stop.

"Daaaamn!" Kato calls, dragging out the exclamation, his voice high-pitched with surprise and admiration—perhaps from being flipped through the air and body slammed into the water. "Where did you learn to do that?"

I think fast. "Self-defense class at the Y," I say, glaring at him. "You scared me! Where did you go?"

"I was trying to surprise you, that was all." Kato bobs over toward me, his grin as wide as ever.

"Well, don't." I continue to glare at him. "You really scared me. I thought you were drowning, and then when you grabbed me. I thought, well, I thought you were, you know, danger."

Kato moves a wet glop of hair out of my face. "I'm sorry. You're right. That wasn't cool of me. I thought it would be funny, but I see now that I was wrong." With his wet hand on my arm, he guides me toward shore and onto a small gravelly area not far from the cliffside. Our feet find bottom, and we climb out, collapsing in the small pebbles and stones. "There. Now neither of us can drown."

"Well, that's unfortunate. I kind of feel like drowning you," I say. My glare has become more of an act. I wasn't mad at him for tricking me, I was mad at myself. How am I supposed to feign innocence when I'm flipping him around in the water like a trained operative?

Kato laughs and lays back, spreading his arms wide, as though he's still in the water, his body lounging on the warm rocks that had been absorbing the sun's heat all day. "Do it then. Get it over with. Tell my father I will miss him," he says with the flair of an over-seasoned actor.

I start laughing, too. "That's not funny," I say with a playful punch in the stomach. He rolls over and scoops me into his arms, smiling at me. I fit like a puzzle piece against him, his mouth resting to the side of my ear as his arms wrap around me, pressing us together. I lean against him. His body heat warms me through my soaking wet clothes.

A sudden sense of dread settles over me. "Please tell me you didn't lose your keys while you were making me think someone killed you."

"They're in my pocket, I swear."

"I thought they were in your hand because they were falling out of your pocket."

"I stuffed them back in my pocket just before we leaped."

I put my arms up around Kato's neck and study him. I had searched the water; I was trained to spot things. I should have been able to see him when he didn't pop to the surface.

But I hadn't.

It makes no sense.

"You okay?" Kato asks.

"With you I am."

His arms pull me closer, and his gaze drops to my lips. He

bites his bottom lip, and goosebumps ripple up my arms. Warmth fills me. So does happiness. I pull his face to mine, kissing him before he has the chance to kiss me. He pulls away and pauses, allowing his breath to feather my lips, before kissing me more deeply. I lose my breath.

I never thought I would find or want something like this when working for Aunt Magdalena was all I thought I ever needed. I know how risky it is, how forbidden it is. I like Kato more than is appropriate for a mission. If my family finds out I like him—as in like, like him—it will all be ripped away from me. I will be sent to Russia to uphold my engagement with Dimitri and marry him when I turn eighteen, if not sooner given the current circumstances.

Leaving Gangster Island no longer holds the appeal it once did.

At the bottom of the cliff, our toes in the cool water, with Kato's arms around me and our lips locked in passion, I am truly at peace. I know I will choose to be stationed in Wisconsin if given the choice. I will choose Kato. He's everything I ever hoped to find in life.

Kato pulls away to breathe and looks at me with the same giddiness I feel. "We should probably head back," he whispers. He sounds out of breath. I know the feeling. "If we want to be back before sundown. We still need to climb back up."

If I return after dark, I can imagine how upset my uncle will be. If I text him from the car, though, it might be okay. So, I ask, "Do we have to go already?"

"No, I guess not. Why? Do you have something in mind?"

"I'd say get a bite to eat, but no restaurant would let us in with our clothes sopping wet."

"I have dry T-shirts in the truck and towels and stuff." Kato lets go of me, and his body heat leaves with him. A sudden chill runs through me.

"That would be great. Next time warn me what we're going

to do so I can bring a change of clothes, yeah?" I follow him toward a winding trail that leads upward.

As we begin our ascent, Kato strings an arm around my shoulders. He places another kiss on my forehead as we make our way up the path back to the parking lot. "Anything for my girlfriend."

RULE 20:

SILENCE IS GOLDEN.

I t takes much longer to climb back up the cliff than it did to plunge downward—obviously. The first few minutes, I don't mind the effort, but then my adrenaline wears off, clouds move in front of the sun, and a wind from the east picks up, chilling me in my wet clothes.

"I guess we should have picked a warmer day," he mutters.

I give him my best semblance of a smile but fall short. "It's fine. Worth the cold." He returns my smile.

When the parking lot comes into view, Kato pulls his keys from his pocket and thumbs the fob to unlock the truck. He turns to me with a devilish grin. "Race you," he says.

"No, Kato. I'm so tired," I say, and then take off sprinting at top speed. My laughter drowns out his reply of shock. I don't know why he's surprised. He knows I like to win.

I beat Kato by a step, my hand slapping the metal of the truck first. The vehicle is still holding the heat from the sun that shone when we first arrived. The truck is filthy, but I hug it anyway to feel its warmth.

"That was a rotten trick," Kato says, but his laugh gives away that he isn't mad. He moves around to the back of the truck. "You're fast. You're a trickster. And you can flip people in the water. Autumn, I'm starting to think you might be a spy."

Panic flashes inside me. Have I been compromised? How could he know? I try to hide my consternation. "Why? Because a girl can't be faster than you?"

Kato shakes his head. "Of course not. It was a joke, Autumn. I didn't mean anything by it." He tosses me a towel. It is gloriously warm from being in the back of the truck. And it's plush, made of piled-thick, high-end cotton. It is not your typical beach towel.

I lean forward, draping the towel over my wet hair before I straighten and wrap it around my head. That's when I see another vehicle in the parking area. "I wonder when they got here," I say, nodding toward a Volkswagen Beetle, as bright and as yellow as the sun. It sits across the gravel lot, but I don't see anyone inside. "They're not cliff-jumping, or we would have run into them. Hiking maybe?"

"Maybe." Kato considers the other vehicle as he pulls out a T-shirt and brings it over to me. "That is one bold car," Kato proclaims, smirking as he hands me the shirt. "Northern Exposure Bar and Restaurant, Phelps," it reads on its front.

Bold for sure, but something feels off about the little, dome-shaped "Bug." That's what my dad calls his Volkswagen Beetle that sits in our garage collecting dust. I shake the concern from my mind. I'm being paranoid. I tell Kato I'm going to change behind a tree.

"You can change in the back of the truck if you want. It has tinted windows in the backseat. No one can see in."

I hesitate for a moment before climbing into the cramped backseat and closing the door behind me. Worried the tint on the windows isn't dark enough, I peel off my wet shirt and drop it on the seat with a splat. I leave on my sports bra even though it's wet, too. I dry my upper body with the towel and put my hair back up in it before pulling the shirt on—yes, warm!—over my head. It's big on me, but not too bad. I grab the hem of the shirt and pull the fabric tight, tying a knot so it's a snugger fit.

That's when I hear a loud "bang!"

A gunshot? Fireworks again?

Either way, it startles me. I fall backward onto the floor of the truck, my eyes widening, every nerve on high alert.

Fireworks don't make sense. There's still too much daylight, even if the skies have clouded over. They wouldn't be visible this time of day. And why would anyone be shooting fireworks in a state park?

Taking a deep breath, I move to the window and peer out. I don't see Kato. I don't see anyone. I wish I had treated this more like a mission and less like a date and brought a knife.

I open the door and hop down, staying light on my feet. When I move around to the front of the truck, I still don't see anyone. Even the sun-yellow Volkswagen is gone. I didn't hear it drive away. Perhaps the bang was the Bug starting up and backfiring.

But then where is Kato?

I focus on my training and try to steady my breathing. My heart hammers in my chest. In such situations, I'm supposed to stay quiet, get low, and get out.

But Kato is missing. He's not here. He wouldn't just leave me. Panic clouds my judgment. Instead of following protocol, I open my mouth, and I do the one thing I know I'm not supposed to.

"KATO!" I scream at the top of my lungs, even though it gives away my position and any cover, or element of surprise. "KATO!"

A faint scream echoes back. "AUTUMN!"

It sounds like it's coming from the cliff.

I take off sprinting and the towel flies off my head, my wet hair whipping behind me, leaving cold, wet slaps on my back. Every step leaves a wet footprint, too. I might as well be a target at a sideshow arcade.

I can't worry about that. I can't worry about being followed —or tracked. Every ounce of training escapes me. I don't even scan my surroundings like I'm supposed to, as fear threatens to seize my throat and strangle every breath out of me.

"KATO!" I scream again, as if we are playing "Marco Polo" with our names. I skid to a stop at the cliff where we had jumped. A small puddle of blood mars the rocky ground.

Oh God!

The cliff is empty. I don't hear Kato respond again.

Bending down, I put my shaking fingers into the blood. It's still warm. Still fresh. I wipe my fingers on my jeans.

I scream Kato's name one more time, my cry echoing across Devils Lake.

I need to focus.

My throat is tight and my stomach drops. My heart pounds, my breath quickens, and my hands hold a slight tremor. I taste blood. I'm chewing on the inside of my cheek. I definitely heard a gunshot. And I definitely heard Kato call back to me. So, he's still in the area, right? And I'm sure he wasn't taken away in the missing Bug. He and whoever is with him must be on foot.

Why would somebody take Kato? Perhaps his dad has ticked off more people than my family.

My eyes search the area, and I discover another splash of blood a few steps down the path we had climbed up. I take off and try to keep my footfalls silent. Rounding a bend, I see Kato's shoes sticking out from behind a rock; I freeze. "Kato?" He doesn't answer. My heart leaps into my throat.

Please, let him be ok. Or maybe it's a trap.

I scan the cliff face toward the clouded sky first but see nothing but trees and branches. I look back over my shoulder at the path I came down. That's clear, too. Everything—except Kato's shoes—is as I recall it from our hike up.

Panic overcomes me. What if it is him and he's hurt? I

don't see any immediate dangers, and my willpower to not rush to him gives out.

I move down to Kato. He's sprawled behind the boulder, unconscious.

I scan the area again before dropping down next to him. I slide fingertips to his wrist and check for a pulse. Finding one, I exhale in relief. I check Kato for a bullet wound and am grateful I don't find one. In fact, he looks unharmed. Just wet and unconscious.

"Kato, you need to wake up," I whisper right into his ear as I pat his cheeks, trying to get him to come to. "Kato, please, get up." As strong as I am, I don't think I can lift him, and if I have to drag him, there's no discreet way for us to leave. A girl dragging an unconscious boy up a cliffside will attract attention. People will be inclined to take note—and pictures—and the possibility is high that they will call the cops.

Kato stirs, and I exhale another sigh of relief.

"Kato," I say, leaning down and pressing my lips to his cheek.

Kato's eyes flutter open, and his hand grabs my arm. "Autumn, you need to run. You need to go. Leave me."

I shake my head. "Absolutely not."

"It's a trap," Kato presses. His eyes are dark with fear. "I heard them talking. They said they want you. Leave *now*. Do as I say. I'll be fine, okay? You need to get out of here now before they hurt you."

"Can you stand?" I ask, refusing to listen to him—or leave him.

"Autumn, watch out!" Kato screams.

An arm wraps around me as something sharp punctures the soft skin of my neck. I try to drive my head back, but my head swims and my vision sways. It feels like getting a shot as a warm burn spreads across my skin before diminishing. I have no idea what's going on, as my mind tries to turn to my training.

My head spins too much to focus. My captor is now the one keeping me upright. My limbs are numb. When I bat at their hand, my attempts at attack are weak brushes. Fear clouds Kato's eyes as a gloved hand jabs him with a needle as well. Kato passes out first. Then my world goes dark.

AUTUMN

AGE 15

C alling Abby led straight to her voicemail, and I cursed before throwing my phone down against the roof of the office building. "I hate my birthday," I grumbled and plopped down, my back pressing against the low wall around the roof's perimeter, hiding me from behind.

My forearm continued to bleed, so I pressed my hand against it. I had tried wrapping it in my sweater, but that hadn't done much except stain my sweater. Alone on the roof, I was freezing cold.

A half hour remained until my birthday was over and I could call to be picked up. I had been hoping Abby would be able to swing by early. It had been 24 hours of hell, but I had done well. What a splendid birthday gift from my parents.

And it would end with me bleeding on the roof of this random office building because I hadn't paid better attention when Mother showed me how to stop a knife wound from bleeding out.

I leaned forward and grabbed my phone, the screen now cracked. I turned it over and over in my hand, a nervous habit.

For my birthday, my parents had gotten me three assassins, which turned into four—my father's touch, I was sure. The first two I eliminated by sunup. Three and four I guessed were recruited within *our family or minor family network. They escaped; they knew my training, my moves, and where I would go.*

No one used real firearms. Just paintball guns. I had lost mine hours earlier when Assassin Number Four pulled out a knife, which he was not supposed to do.

If I hit them with a paintball three times, they were out. If I got hit once, I was out—dead. All I had gotten so far were four attackers and a nasty knife wound.

I had gotten to higher ground in hopes of being helicoptered out.

I had already escaped them, and I was so tired. I should have been allowed to pull out.

Unless...

My eyes snapped back into focus. I caught sight of the paintball gun across the roof and leaped into a shoulder roll. A splatter of paint hit the low wall where I had been sitting.

I took off running across the roof, my feet fast, my footing sure. Reaching the end of the roof I jumped, sailing through the air for a moment before landing on the next roof.

Protecting my wounded arm, I didn't want to roll and tried not to risk getting roof gravel in the wound. This proved to be an error as my ankle turned on impact and I fell to the ground. I bit my tongue to keep myself from screaming out in pain. Getting up, I limped, moving as fast as I could.

Winning was going to be a lot harder with a hurt arm and a rolled ankle, but I wasn't done yet.

Not yet.

RULE 21:

DON'T HESITATE.

"Shhh." At the sound of Kato's voice, my eyes flutter open. I emerge from the darkness of unconsciousness—like coming out of a deep sleep—to the darkness of wherever it is we are. Kato's arms are around me, comforting me.

We've been kidnapped.

I must have been sloppy. I must have somehow led someone to us, and now Kato is in danger right along with me.

But if the main threat to my family is Kato's dad, why are we both trapped in the dark?

I blink, opening my eyes wider, but it is too dark to see anything. My hand presses against Kato's shirt, still damp from the swim. His heartbeat pounds away, like a drum roll. He is terrified, and it is all my fault.

"Where are we?" I mumble to him. My head feels light. It's like all my pain has been wiped clean. I feel it returning, reality setting back in as whatever I was hit with fades from my system.

"It's okay, I'm here," Kato whispers into my ear as he holds me tighter, his hand rubbing my back. With his hands bound together, his soothing rubs are clumsy. "They brought us here. I think we're in a warehouse, but it's hard to tell. They drugged me when you were changing. I had my gun in the truck bed, but they were faster than me. I'm so sorry, Autumn. You should have listened to me and left. They know our real names. They said them. And then, of course, we were yelling them."

"Can we get out?" I ask.

Kato shakes his head. "There are two guards outside the only exit. They've talked a couple times. Nothing exciting." Kato leans down and presses a kiss against my forehead. "Just focus on me. I'll get us out of this. I did hear them mention my dad, so this has to be about him. Autumn, I'm so sorry I got you dragged into this."

"It's okay," I mutter, my mind working on ways to disarm the two guards without getting us both killed. My uncle likes to use a move called the Power Light, but I'm not sure I'm agile enough to pull it off in my current state. My head remains swimmy from the drug that sent me to La La Land.

"No, it's not okay," Kato argues. "I'm going to protect you though, okay? Whatever they want from my dad, we'll figure it out."

I want to tell him not to worry because I've been in situations like this before, but I need to keep my family's secrets closely guarded.

Maybe I could use this moment as the perfect excuse to tell him everything.

"I'm okay, Kato," I say instead. "We're okay. We're in this together."

My hands fumble against the ropes rubbing against my wrists. I know this knot. There's only one idiot I associate an English Cream Soda Knot with; the smirk on my face grows. Within seconds I'm free. "Hey, they didn't really tie me," I say in the dark and lean closer to Kato. I untie his hands, too. We both untie our own legs.

"They probably didn't see you as much of a threat," Kato mutters. I barely hear him, and I wish I hadn't. I know that

RULE 25: DON'T FALL FOR THE TARGET

I'm supposed to come off to him as non-threatening—a normal girl trapped in a bad situation. But his words still sting. As soon as he is free, he wraps his arms around me. "They must be after me. Do you know any self-defense?"

Let's see, I'm a black belt in three forms of martial arts. "A little," I say.

"Okay. I don't want to risk it. I'm not bad, but if they have a gun or any weapons..." he trails off and grimaces. "If anything happened to you Autumn, I wouldn't be able to forgive myself."

In the darkness, I'm able to make out the lines of his face. I place a hand on his cheek and bring his lips to mine, kissing him deeply. Kato's hands wrap around my waist, pulling me onto his lap and close to him. His lips are gentler than they had been when we were in the water, like he is savoring having me with him.

My hand slides off his cheek and presses against his wet shirt. I wish we hadn't both left our phones in the car. I pull away from Kato, searching his face, unsure if he can see mine. "We're going to be okay," I promise.

If Quinton is behind this, like I suspect he is based off the knot, we aren't in any real danger. In fact, I know my overprotective brother rather well. I sit back against Kato's lap and look around. As I suspect, a faint, red light glows in what I assume is the upper corner of the warehouse, or wherever it is we are being held.

"There's a camera," I tell him and point at it in the dark.

"They can see us then," Kato says. "Do you think that's a good sign or a bad sign?"

"They can probably hear us, too." Quinton likes cameras with mics, and those always have the red light, as long as they're the quality and brand Dad approves of. Typically, Quinton would be yelled at to cover the light, so it isn't visible. Either my parents aren't here, or they're distracted.

"I'm going to say a camera is bad news," Kato answers his

own question. "Maybe we should stop making out if they're watching us. It's kind of creepy."

I ignore his rambling and focus on our escape as I run my hand against the floor. My fingertips brush cool metal. I stand up, putting my hand out, and use the red light as a guide from what I suspect is a corner to the adjoining side wall. I find that we are in a much smaller space than the darkness led me to believe. Kato remains seated against the opposite wall, and it only takes me a couple of steps to join him on the floor.

"I think we're in a shipping container," I say. "You're probably right. It's in a warehouse or some other large open space, and they're using the shipping container as a type of cell to lock us up."

"If only we knew who they were. Look, my dad deals with some sketchy characters in his business. It's probably just a ransom situation."

"Just a ransom? Do you get kidnapped a lot?" I ask, putting a knee on either side of him, so that I sit on his lap facing him. His arms curl around my waist. "As your girlfriend, should I get used to dates ending like this?"

Kato chuckles. "I hope not."

"Maybe they're after me," I throw out as I lean my face close to his, so the curve of his face and features become more visible in the dark. "You said something like that before you passed out on the hillside. They're probably looking for someone who is good at ungracefully falling into water."

"Doubtful," he muses. I hear a smile in his voice.

His heart calms under my hand as I lean closer. Our lips touch once again. He leans forward, but I pull back, teasing. "I thought the camera creeped you out."

"I think they are after you," Kato says. "They need someone with a sharp wit who enjoys torturing men."

"I do enjoy torturing you."

"Just don't go falling for any of the other guys you're torturing. You're *my* girlfriend."

"I wouldn't dream of it," I say, as my lips meet his. His hands pull me closer. I slide up until our torsos meet, my legs wrapping around his back, my hand running through his hair.

Kato pulls away and I let out a sound of protest. "Do you hear that?" he whispers.

I hear it now—the scratch of metal. The doors begin to slide open. Light pours inside.

I get off Kato's lap and sit next to him in the container. As the light pours in, it reveals the red light in the corner is the camera I suspected it to be.

Kato's hand finds mine, and I squeeze it as he gets to his feet and helps me up to mine. The long hem of his T-shirt I borrowed falls down around me. The knot I tied at the bottom to make it look like it fit properly has come undone. The shirttail is nothing but wrinkles.

The light becomes blinding, and I can't see anything as the door continues to scrape open. But I do get a good look at Kato. He's squinting, his free hand held up in front of his face to block the light. His hair sticks out at odd angles where I had been running my fingers through it. We were the sort of mess that would lead nuns to pray for our souls.

The door finishes opening, and two masked figures come into the container, one grabbing Kato, the other grabbing me. They push us outside.

I had been spot on about the shipping container, but Kato was off about the warehouse. We're in the middle of a school gymnasium. How they managed to get the large shipping container in here, I have no idea.

My thought is cut short as I am pulled one way and Kato the other. They're splitting us up, not taking us somewhere together.

"Kato!" I yell, as I try to fight off my kidnapper.

"Autumn!" Kato yells back and elbows his captor hard in the gut.

"Shut up," my brother's voice hisses in my ear as he

continues to pull me away. "You've caused enough of a scene already."

I look back over at Kato, trying to look as frightened as possible to keep my cover. Two more captors join us so that it's now three people holding Kato back and dragging him away. He continues yelling for me before vanishing behind the bleachers.

Quinton drags me out of the gym and into what appears to be an outer entryway.

"Are you going to be stupid?" he asks and stops outside the gymnasium doors.

I push him off me. "Will you take off that ridiculous mask?" I ask.

Quinton does, his red hair flying free, and glares at me. "Sorry. We didn't want your *boyfriend* to recognize us."

"What the hell is going on? What are you even doing here? Why did you kidnap us? I was doing perfectly fine." I cross my arms.

"Yeah, you were really on track to get an STD. What was that in there? Do you actually like him?"

"That was me knowing that it was my idiot brother in charge and realizing the fastest way out of the shipping container was putting on a little show by making out with Kato." I artfully dodge his question. "Now, why did you kidnap us?"

"We hadn't planned to, but then you went off the radar, and stopped answering your phone, so we followed protocol to retrieve you. Then your *boyfriend* pulled out a gun and fired at us, so we had to neutralize him, which we couldn't do without blowing your cover. Or kidnapping you as well," Quinton explains.

I shake my head. "Kato told me he was attacked and didn't have time to get a weapon."

"He lied to you."

"He wouldn't do that," I defend, and my brother raises his

eyebrow. "What did you need me so badly for anyway? Just missed my beautiful face?"

"Maybe if you had one I would."

I sock my brother in the arm hard, and he laughs.

"Actually, you have bigger issues today. Dad's with me. And he brought your fiancé."

"My who now?" My mouth drops open. "Dimitri is here? In Wisconsin?" My brain steps on the gas pedal as thoughts come faster than I can process them. Dimitri is here. I have met Dimitri once. I'm supposed to marry him. Is he here to marry me? What about Kato? I don't even know Dimitri. I lost his hat. What if he wants his hat back? He doesn't want his hat back, he wants to marry me. Oh shit. I can't get married!

Quinton nods. "Apparently, if you won't go to Russia, Russia will come to you. And Russia isn't happy you were kissing another guy."

"You make it sound like I cheated on Russia."

"That's because to them, you cheated on Russia. You cheated on Russia with a Wisconsin boy."

RULE 22:

A SENSE OF HUMOR CAN GET YOU KILLED.

Quinton leads me out the gym doors and into the parking lot, where I spot Kato's truck. How considerate of my family to think to move it—while kidnapping us. Quinton leads me back to the front doors of the building.

"Why did we go outside to get back inside?" I ask.

"It's quicker. Part of the old roof caved in last winter under the snow." Quinton pulls off the plywood blocking the entrance. He holds the door open for me. What a gentleman.

We barely talk. I'm like a prisoner being led to Old Sparky, my last day on death row. I know what awaits me won't be that bad, but I will get a good yelling at. How can they tell me I may be stationed wherever I want if they expect me to leave with Dimitri? It isn't fair. I should at least be allowed to complete my first solo mission without interference.

Of course, that isn't what I am mad about.

Quinton leads me through the school cafeteria. All the tables and chairs are gone, but the long window with a counter is a dead giveaway of the cavernous space's former use. Spray-painted graffiti covers the walls, and empty beer cans litter the floor.

"Did you throw a bachelor party?" I tease Quinton, kicking one of the cans. He doesn't answer, and I realize I'm not the only one who's angry.

Quinton leads me to Room 108 and opens the door. I step inside the old classroom, recognizing only a few of the faces glaring at me. Quinton closes the door behind us.

"Hi guys." I attempt a small smile.

Father moves through the group, stops in front of me, and does something unexpected. He pulls me into a hug. My whole body tenses, unsure how to react until he whispers his true intentions in my ear, "We will discuss this further later." He wanted to do was give me a scold warning, but not in a way everyone could hear.

He pulls away but holds my shoulders at arm's length as if inspecting me. I look around the room, taking in each judgy, unsmiling face. I assume most of them came with the Daxterovs, but the only Daxterova I recognize is Dimitri's mom. Married to the head of the Daxterov family, I have met her before, even if she has kept her son away from me. She hovers above everyone and wears heels as tall as Ashlynn's. Her dark hair pools around her shoulders as she takes a long look at me. She drenches me with an icy glare; my chilly trek up the cliffside earlier seems like a sweat in the sauna. Ashlynn, my father, Quinton, and I are the only Alderidges, I note.

"Он баловал свою дочь, и посмотрите, какой она оказалась," Dimitri's mother speaks to the man standing behind her. Her words sting. A folding table sits in front of a monitor on the opposite wall. Because it's playing the footage from inside the storage container, I know Dimitri's mom had a front-row seat to my antics.

"I turned out just fine, thank you, Mrs. Daxterova. My father doesn't coddle me."

Mrs. Daxterova raises her eyebrows. "She speaks Russian?" Her American accent is perfect. Perhaps she is an American, too, who married into the Daxterovs like I'm set to do.

"я свободно говорю. When you're engaged to a Russian, you tend to take the time to learn the language so your in-laws can't speak ill of you behind your back right to your face," I explain.

"Autumn..." my father warns.

I'm so sick of everyone treating me like a little kid. I can handle my own mission. I should be able to make my own decisions. "Can someone please tell me what is going on?" As I scan the room, I realize I don't see Dimitri, though Quinton had said he was here.

"What is going on is that we came all the way to Wisconsin, at your father's request, just so we could watch my son's supposed future wife kissing another boy inside of a shipping container." Mrs. Daxterova's voice is level and calm, like a lawyer laying out the facts, but I can tell she isn't happy with me—or my father.

I widen my stance. "If someone had told me the plan ahead of time, I would have adjusted my actions accordingly."

"What I don't understand is why, after you saw the camera, you still insisted on kissing that boy, and sitting in his lap, and God knows what else, knowing full well someone was watching. Is being a tramp an American thing?"

"It seems both families are losing their civility today," my father interjects. "Let's all try and remember who we are and who we are speaking to."

When no one else speaks, I realize it is still my turn. I'm not supposed to speak. Being put on the spot, and my father's words, cool my anger into nerves. "My objective was to be released from the shipping container as quickly as possible without blowing my cover, since I was not informed of any kidnapping plan. Any attempt to break out of the container ran the risk of the target asking questions I wouldn't know how to answer. There is only so much that can be brushed away by saying you took a class at the Y. By kissing Kato—my target, I mean—I knew my brother would see and open the door and get a move on. It looks like I was correct."

Mrs. Daxterova raises an eyebrow again. "So, you were playing everyone involved? Including your very own family members?"

"Yes, ma'am."

Mrs. Daxterova's glare turns into a smile, and when she lets out a laugh, from deep within her gut, her fellow Russians join her. "Clever, clever girl. I like you. We need fire like that in Russia. Mr. Alderidge, why did you not tell my beautiful future daughter-in-law the plan so she wouldn't have to kiss that thing you have her following around?"

That thing? A wave of anger crashes over me. Kato is not a dung beetle. He is a sweet boy who has been nothing but kind to me. I am playing him, too. But I hold my tongue.

"Our intention was not to have you arrive and be faced with this mess. Today's actions were formulated and executed quickly. Autumn's phone went off the grid. We were worried Autumn had been made. Before losing signal, she had been driving for three hours to an undisclosed location with her target. After failing to get in contact with her, we decided action had to be taken. We regret the unfortunate circumstances surrounding your arrival."

"Hm. Yes. Most unfortunate. However, it is clear to me, and it should be clear to you, that Autumn is still very much needed on this mission. We cannot take her back to Russia right now."

"What?" my father and I say at the same time, though our surprise is for different reasons.

I was a child last time I was in Russia. I remember the hotel lobby's plate of free, fresh-baked chocolate chip cookies the best from the trip. A little sign said to take one, but I was allowed to take two, even though it was almost dinner time, since I had read the sign despite it being in Russian. Not having to return so soon floods me with relief and gratitude for Mrs. Daxterova.

"Yes, I think it's clear you need her here," Mrs. Daxterova reassures with a nod of her head. "Your target trusts and loves her completely. It's almost adorable. She is needed here to complete this mission. He may be male, but even he wouldn't accept it if Autumn vanished, and we plunked your niece down in her place. Sometimes I think you forget: All people have feelings, Michael."

People rarely refer to my father by his first name. I look up at him, expecting him to be outraged and, I assume, disrespected. Being contradicted should spark anger in him. But he doesn't appear mad at all. In fact, he seems to consider her words. "I think you're right, Mrs. Daxterova," he says. "I'm sorry you came all this way, only to turn back."

"We're not turning back," Mrs. Daxterova snorts back with a sneer that makes my skin crawl.

My father raises his eyebrow at the woman. "Oh?"

"Certainly not. You still need help, don't you? And Dimitri and Autumn should get to know each other, on an unofficial basis of course."

"Of course."

"If they are to be married, it is only right. Besides, Russia is not as close as one might think. I certainly don't want to start another eleven-hour plane ride today. We're staying." In her heels, she's a few inches taller than my father. "Now, how are we going to send Autumn back to her target without blowing her cover?"

I can't look like I went and had a nice chat. I glance at Quinton for support, but his face says this is my own fault.

"We already have a plan in place for that," my father assures. He knows the importance of me keeping my cover.

"You're going to have to beat me up, aren't you?" I ask with a distasteful tone, my head dropping. Understandably, I'm not excited.

AUTUMN

AGE 12

At the sound of my parents' voices, I hurried down the stairs, Quinton close behind. We were supposed to be asleep and in bed, but I had been awakened by a smashing sound and my parents talking loudly. They sounded angry, but not at each other. A shared anger.

I stopped halfway down the stairs, ducking behind the railing. If it wasn't dark, I knew I would be spotted instantly. Instead, I was able to watch my parents who were in the parlor.

"Why was he even in New Zealand?" Dad asked. "He was supposed to be in Warsaw. We sent him to Warsaw!"

"Apparently, he was following a lead." Mother slumped into the plush sofa, putting her hand over her face. "He was so well-trained. This shouldn't have happened."

My father sat down next to her and took her hand in his. "What do you want us to do? I will send an army if that's what it takes. It's your call, though. He's your brother."

I looked up at Quinton crouched next to me. He seemed as in the dark as we both literally were. I never liked not knowing what was happening.

My mother had one sibling, an older brother; they were the same age difference as Quinton and me. I had never met him, and even *though our parents insisted Quinton knew him, Quinton also had no memories of our uncle.*

"No," my mother finally breathed. "It should be Jenna's decision. She didn't call me to ask for help. She called to let me know what happened. She knew if she wanted the resources, we would have provided. But she didn't ask. We can't pull him out without her go-ahead. He's her operative, not ours. And we didn't send him anywhere, Michael. We strongly encouraged him to be stationed in Warsaw."

My father shook his head. "I'm so sorry this is happening."

"It could happen to any of us. Getting your cover blown isn't as rare in the minor families as it is in the majors. You have the resources to buy lies—and to leave the second things start heading south. We don't."

"You mean, they don't," my father corrected. "You're an Alderidge now."

"That didn't help my brother when they realized he was a spy planning to rob them blind. Why he even went on a mission like that, I don't know. If they needed money, we could have helped them. They didn't need to..." My mother trailed off.

"What is it?"

"Someone is watching us. I think the kids are out of bed."

I looked up at Quinton, whose wide-eyed stare mirrored my own. We both tore up the stairs and back to our bedrooms before we could get busted. Rule one: don't get caught.

RULE 23:

LET THEM UNDERESTIMATE YOU.

I sit in a dark classroom tied to a chair, limp against my restraints. Quinton assured me it will be impossible for Kato to miss me. He joked that maybe Kato would leave me behind and escape by himself if given the chance. I punched him in the arm for that, harder than the last time. Even in jest, the suggestion upsets me. The longer I sit in the dark, though, the more I wonder if I am the one who has been getting played all along.

This time Quinton hadn't been the one to tie me, and, despite trying, I'm unable to get the knots undone. Eventually someone will need to free me.

When he discovered I needed to be beat up, Quinton had become extremely upset by this entire plan and had gone off with Father to "discuss things," which I know means he wants this scheme called off. I would have done the same if the roles were reversed. Still, I wish my brother could see I have the ability to complete this mission.

One of the Daxterovs men hit me a few times in the face, apologizing each time. Mrs. Daxterova had used her diamond ring to cut what turned out to be a shallow scratch across my cheek. They added a bit of makeup to make the wounds appear more gruesome. I think I look worse than I feel as I slump in the wooden chair, waiting for Kato.

I hope he doesn't look as bad as I do. No one would tell me what they planned to do to him. Father said it was for the best if I was in the dark, because then my reactions would be more believable. He had given me another awkward hug before leaving me to be tied up. It was his idea to turn out the lights. I wish there was at least a night-light.

I had been instructed not to talk, either, because Kato was in the room nearby. I haven't heard him. I wonder if he heard me. The Russian simulated the sounds of a struggle and cued me when to scream out in pain.

I hate this.

I hate lying.

I hate pretending.

If I heard Kato screaming like that, I know how I would feel, and I'm not even supposed to like him. But I do as my family says, as though I am on autopilot. And now I am alone in silence and darkness.

The faint creak of a door echoes in the hallway. I pray it is Kato coming to look for me—or escaping himself.

My door bursts open. A figure stands in the doorway backlit and silhouetted by the light streaming from outside. I raise my head, as though it takes great effort, and look up at whoever it is. "I'm sorry," I mutter, though I'm not sure why I'm apologizing.

The figure flies into the room and drops down on a knee next to me, a look of pain on his untouched face. *Thank God, he's okay.*

Kato cups my cheek in his hand and, seeing the condition I'm in, recoils. Is he surprised? Or worried about hurting me more? I lean my head into his hand.

"Kato, they told me you would leave me if you had the chance," I say, closing my eyes. It isn't a lie, even if Quinton meant it as a joke. My eyelids flutter and Kato's face twists from pain to anger.

"I would never leave you," he assures. "We need to be quiet." He then gets to work untying me. He succeeds with remarkable speed. In under a minute, I am free from my binds. Kato kneels in front of me again and throws the ropes away, pushing his hair out of his face. "How bad is it?"

"They only hit me in the face. I think I'm okay. How did you get out?"

"They left my door unlocked. I was able to use the edge of a metal table in my room to cut through my binds. I'm fine, really," he says, brushing aside my concern. "Do you know who they are? Or where they are now?"

I hesitate. The tone in his voice is not what I expect. It is as if he is asking me because he wants to know if he has to be the one to tell me. "They were masked," is all I say.

Kato nods and helps me to my feet.

We hurry through the halls. I let Kato guide me as we move, even though I know the way out better than he does. He keeps doubling back, cursing under his breath as he holds my hand tight. Quinton wasn't joking about the roof. Fallen debris blocks most of the hallways. The holes create an open concept school. If they weren't letting us escape, we would have been caught the moment we stepped into the hallway.

"Kato, wait," I say, stopping him. "What if we cut through the gym?"

Kato shakes his head. "There's no way it's empty. It's also really exposed."

It is supposed to be empty exactly for this reason. "Can we please just try? I'm feeling dizzy." That isn't a lie, either. Being punched in the face, even just for looks, hurts like crazy, and it has thrown off my balance and left me a bit woozy.

Kato turns to me and brushes a hand over my cheek, debating options. "Of course. Of course, we can try," he says after a moment. He takes my hand once more, guiding me as we make our way to the gym doors. Kato peeks through the window into the gym and nods at me before he pulls the door open.

The high-pitched "SCREEECH!" from its aged hinges makes me wince and jump. A piercing alarm—aren't those supposed to be turned off?—wails, too.

"Can you run?" Kato yells over the alarm.

I shrug my shoulders. I'm honestly not sure. Without hesitating, Kato scoops me into his arms. I give a yelp in surprise, wrapping my arms around his neck while my head continues to swim. Kato runs faster than when he had raced me to the truck—and he hadn't been carrying anything then.

On the other side of the gym, near the doors, Kato comes to an abrupt stop and puts me down, my feet thumping against the hard wooden floor. As I catch my balance, a masked figure steps between us and the exit that, as I recall, goes to a lobby area. Beyond that, Kato's truck is parked.

Kato lunges at the masked figure, his fist colliding square with their nose. The figure tries sweeping Kato's legs, but Kato jumps over them and lands in a superhero crouch, using the low vantage point to launch his shoulder up into the attacker's midsection at full force. Kato drives him into the doorjamb. "How dare you hurt her," Kato growls in the attacker's face.

"Kato, let's go," I say, moving to the door. "There will be others."

Kato looks at me before turning back to the attacker. He rips off the attacker's mask. A dazed expression covers my stupid brother's face. Then he glares at Kato. "Listen to Cinderella, Bulldog," Quinton sneers.

Kato punches Quinton in the gut—hard—and Quinton doubles over.

"Kato!" I say, grabbing his hand and pulling him away, "we need to go."

But Kato hesitates, confusion washing over his face. "That's... that guy, he's the one from paintball."

"Please, let's go."

"Why is the guy from paintball here?"

Quinton staggers to his feet, and I curse. He should stay down. This isn't a real fight. According to the plan, we are supposed to go; we are supposed to win this fight. There's not supposed to be sirens or fighting. Did Quinton forget? He steps in our way again.

"Step aside," Kato sneers.

"You step aside, away from her," Quinton threatens. Kato's arm squeezes tighter around me.

"You're in bad shape. Let us go," I yell at my brother.

"I'm in fine shape, Barf Breath," Quinton barks. And then my brother does the stupidest thing I have ever seen him do, which is saying something. He pulls out his knife, its blade glinting in the dim illumination from the gymnasium's overhead fluorescents.

"Autumn, please get behind me," Kato instructs, not taking his eyes off the weapon. He lets go of me. I move to his side but don't step behind him.

My brother lunges at Kato, the blade extended. Kato jumps out of the way just in time. He grabs Quinton's arm as it swings past, but it's a mistake. Quinton uses the leverage of Kato's grip to jump up and kick both his feet square into Kato's chest. They both fall to the floor.

Quinton gets back up first, but the split second he has before Kato jumps up isn't enough time for a counterattack. They square off, Quinton pointing the blade gripped in his hand.

"How long have you been following us?" Kato asks Quinton as they dance around each other, like boxers unwilling to make the first move. They're playing a dangerous game of chicken.

Quinton doesn't answer. His mouth curves into a scowl.

"Do you live around Phelps? I never saw you before that

day at paintball. Did you follow us all the way down here today? Why? What is going on?"

Kato keeps circling while asking his distracting questions until his back is to the exit, and he's back standing by me. In one swift move, he turns like a cheetah, grabs my arm, and pulls me through the doors. Quinton's blade embeds into the old door as we bolt past it, and Kato pauses, jerking me to stop as well. Slowing, Kato reaches up and touches his ear. His fingers return red and sticky. Quinton nicked him, a completely unnecessary thing to do. Stupid idiot brother!

"Let's keep moving," I yell to Kato.

But Kato isn't listening. He lets go of my hand, returns to the door, pulls the knife from the wood, and turns back to face my brother. He turns the blade over in his palm, and a malicious grin forms on his face, one I've never seen before.

"You shouldn't have let go of your weapon, Carrot Head."

Quinton had thrown the knife and missed on purpose. I don't think Kato will return the favor.

Kato moves toward my brother, knife in hand, and Quinton stands his ground, waiting for him. In a split second of horror, I realize Quinton intends to fight without a weapon against Kato with a knife.

"Kato, no!" I say grabbing the arm holding the knife. "He isn't worth it! Please, let's go!"

Kato shakes me off. "He's going to keep coming for us, Autumn. I have no idea why. But I do know that we need to finish this fight. What better time than now?"

"No, he's not going to keep coming after us! We don't need to do anything but leave!"

Kato looks down at me. "You know him, don't you." He doesn't say it as a question but as a statement. A flicker of realization flashes across his features.

Fear fills me. I feel like a bunny in a live trap. "Please, let's just go."

Kato nods, folding the knife closed and pocketing it. He follows me as we hurry out of the school.

My cover is blown. I know it.

Stupid Quinton!

My cover is blown. But I have no choice except follow Kato to his truck, where his keys wait on the driver's seat. He doesn't question how the truck or the keys got where they are. With a humorless scoff, he hops in, and we leave. Kato stomps the accelerator to the floor with his foot using every ounce of anger he can muster.

———

KATO SPEEDS NORTH. We barely talk. As we leave farm country for the forested Northwoods, I keep a watch out for deer. If we hit one at this speed, we will be in serious trouble. Ashlynn had told me that sometimes deer spring out of nowhere, but I'm not about to tell Kato to slow down. We've escaped a kidnapping, my cover is blown, and if there is ever a time for speeding, it's now.

"That was your family, wasn't it?" Kato says, and I swear my heart stops for a moment.

"What?" I delay with a question and look over at him, forgetting the danger of a deer. Right now, I'm the deer, praying I don't get run over.

Kato pounds his fist against the steering wheel. The truck picks up speed over a hill and down the other side. "I'm so stupid," he says, his tone contrite. But I hear something else in his voice, the same lilt I heard on the cliff earlier.

He has been covering up an accent. It is slight, but there. "The redhead, that's why he was at paintball. He's been tailing you, making sure I don't try anything, right? Cousin of yours or something?" Kato's voice is angry. He may not be as in the dark as we think. If it came to it, could I fight him? Would I?

"Kato..." I trail off, not sure what to say.

"Well, no wonder you're terrified of them. What kind of effed-up family kidnaps their own? That's why you didn't want to leave Devils Lake and hurry back. I wouldn't either if my family treated me like that." His accent is Norwegian, I think, but placing accents while my heart rate accelerates leaves plenty of room for error.

Abby would know. She would have knocked Kato out and commandeered the vehicle by now, too.

I should attack Kato. It makes sense, doesn't it?

But I can't.

Then I hear his words again in my head. I look at him, no longer with fear but with sudden realization. He thinks I'm scared of my family. I can use that. *Rule twenty-three: let them underestimate you.*

"I don't know," I say, and I force my bottom lip to quiver. "Kato, your voice? Please don't tell me you're a liar, like them." I mentally cross my fingers hoping this works, and that he doesn't nose-dive the truck into a lake and leave me to die while he swims out and frames it as an accident.

Kato looks over at me, and I realize his anger isn't directed at me at all. It's *for* me. His eyes hold a bead of pity as he watches me like I'm a wounded animal. His voice is soft, as if he's worried he might spook me when he speaks again. "Autumn, I am nothing like them. I'm going to protect you, whatever the cost."

"What do you mean?"

"How much do you know about your family's business?" Kato asks.

Sure, he'll protect me, but at the cost of information about my family. Nothing comes free in this business. I guess I should know that by now. Somehow, I'm not even surprised.

I don't want to lie to him anymore, but I know that trusting him is also the wrong move. "My parents own an international business. It's a family business, so pretty much my whole extended family is involved. We travel a lot, and my dad keeps saying that someday he'll train me to take over." If he thinks Quinton is a cousin, that means the real future head of the family is safe. Kato must not know everything. I'm not about to give my brother over to him.

"You're the eldest child?"

"I'm the only child."

"And they sent you here?"

"They said it would be safer. Kato, what's going on?"

"Autumn, your family isn't looking out for you. I am. And I'm taking you back to my house. You can hide there for as long as you want. We have plenty of room. My dad runs our family, and your parents run yours, and yes, it's an international business. Your family runs a mafia. And my family is trying to stop it."

"What?" I make my voice sound surprised, even a little panicked.

"You seriously know none of this?" Kato demands. He takes his eyes off the road for a moment as he reaches out and takes my hand in his. "If they want you to take over, why wouldn't they have told you by now?"

"I—I don't know," I stumble. He's right. It would have made more sense for me to go against them than pretend to know nothing. But it's too late to change stories if I want Kato to continue to believe me.

Kato nods, apparently buying the lie. "Okay. Well, you can't go back to where they hit you. That's not okay. My family isn't perfect, either, but we don't beat our own. We were part of the major crime families in the 1960s."

"Crime families..." I repeat as if I'm dazed. I need to play along.

Kato nods. "But your family—your grandparents—turned on us and broke any sort of peace deal we had. In one night, they struck every member of our family, taking us out."

"My family killed your family?"

"They slaughtered everyone except my grandmother. She

managed to escape, and she kept the family going. We got powerful enough to, you know, return the favor. And I guess your family has decided to strike back against me by hurting you, which is really low considering you are their family."

I nod; it's starting to make sense. This is why we were under attack. One child survived. The rumors were true. My family is being picked off, our bases going dark, for something none of us were a part of.

"How far are we from your place? I don't like being on the road. They know your truck," I say. Perhaps the kidnapping idea had been a good one, even if I hadn't understood it. It is leading me to where I need to be. Or, where my family wants me to be.

Kato glances at me, that pained look in his eyes again. "We're almost there. And don't worry. When I'm done, your family won't be able to hurt you, or anyone else ever again."

This is not usually how it goes when your cover gets blown. They kill you, hold you for ransom, torture you or throw you in jail. In the case of my mother's brother, it was all four, though not in that order. For me, getting my cover blown has been helpful to the mission. He's taking me to his house.

"Did you know who I was when I first docked in Phelps?" I ask.

"Yes. Well, no. Kind of. I recognized the pontoon as the same one always docked at Gangster Island. We can see your dock from our property. I didn't know who you were, but I knew you were linked to the Alderidge family. I never would have guessed, though, that you're next in line."

"Why not?" I ask. I believe I could be a leader. It's a little insulting that he thinks I couldn't.

"I startled you by standing near your boat. Most heads of families aren't that jumpy that they would fall in the lake." Kato smiles. "Why did you come to Phelps that day?"

"I was looking for you," I blurt out without thinking. "My cousin said you were a good person that I maybe should befriend, because I didn't know anyone but her. But then I met you, and I thought you were an arrogant pig. I don't think that anymore," I add.

Kato cuts me a side eye—I am so blowing this. Yes, Autumn, insult the guy who is driving you to his house. Great plan.

"I was really lonely and needed a friend since I'm stuck here while my family goes to Peru, so. So, I guess they wanted me to get close to you for some reason? Oh gosh, what else have they been lying to me about? I'm so sorry, Kato."

Kato shakes his head. "It's fine. I'm glad they did. Your cousin's Mary, right?"

I want to say no, but that would be an obvious lie. "Yep."

"Good thing she rejected Seb then," Kato says.

"I didn't know she rejected Seb."

"Not everyone is as lucky as us." He holds his hand out, palm up on the middle console for me to take. With a smile and a pang of guilt in my chest, I slide my hand into his. Our fingers interlock as we ride in silence through twisting forested hills.

Kato turns into a driveway and stops the truck at a gate. He has to lean out to enter the code. I watch closely and commit it to memory: "72D13." The gate swings open.

We drive through and head down a dirt path. Men and women in camouflage with rifles hide in wooden perches in the trees. I can't come back this way without Kato. A fresh wave of panic sets—I'm going to be trapped here.

"Don't worry," Kato assures. "No one will hurt you here. No one will ever hurt you again."

If I run, I kind of doubt that.

I feel like a lost rescue dog being brought home for the first time, not someone's girlfriend and certainly not an operative who's supposed to be in control of her mission. All I need is for him to reach over, scratch behind my ear, and call me a good girl.

Kato parks the car in the driveway, and this time I don't jump out before he walks over to my side. I let him open my door for me and help me down. My head throbs. Speeding around curves and up and down hills through the Northwoods took its toll.

"You look pale," Kato says, his eyes pinched with concern.

There's more security here than my family thought. Two people carrying machine guns stand on either side of a grand, white-washed wooden double door. He leads me up the tiled outdoor path past them and then inside and across marble floors. The mansion makes me think of a summer home in the Hamptons, not a quaint lakeside cabin in tiny Conover, Wisconsin. Everything inside is white, except the black railing on the grand staircase swooping up to my left as I walk in. No coats hang by the door, no boots line up in a row. Just sterile white marble.

"I'm not feeling good," I admit. A man in a fine suit closes the door behind us and helps Kato out of his jacket. "You have a butler?"

Without answering, Kato guides me to a green velvet chair that occupies a large portion of the entryway and has me sit. "You're okay now," he says. "I have to tell my dad you're here. Especially since you're an Alderidge, we can't let your presence in the house be a surprise. If he runs into you, he might think you broke in rather than being my guest. Of course, he will be surprised that you're here at all. But I'll deal with him. You don't need to worry about that."

Kato turns to the butler: "Please prepare a room with a private bathroom for Autumn. She needs rest." The butler nods and leaves.

Kato kisses the top of my head and then vanishes up the grand winding staircase and out of view.

Besides the snipers lining the driveway, I don't identify much security in the house. I stand and rub my cheek where Mrs. Daxterova cut me with her ring. Dried blood flakes off onto the white marble floor. In front of me, two doors and bump-outs bottleneck between where I am and what appears to be a kitchen and living room. Straight through, a large deck stretches to the bank of the lake beyond that. The view is amazing—and, oh goodness, it faces my uncle's home. They have an excellent view of it. Why no one had ever pointed it out to me is a mystery.

I open a set of closed doors on my left before I reach the living room and kitchen and find an all-white marble bathroom bigger than some of the rustic cabins lining the lake. Even the wooden cabinets are painted white. Everything feels so empty, so cold and foreboding. I prefer homey. I can't imagine living somewhere like this, even for the summer.

Inside the bathroom I go to the medicine cabinet and find Tylenol. I pop three in my mouth and swallow them dry. Closing the cabinet, I'm startled by my reflection.

My heart skips a beat, and I gasp.

The girl in the mirror stands there, silent and still. And a mess. Her nose is bloodied, and rivulets of blood stain her T-shirt like small rivers. A cut makes a red line across her cheek.

I had forgotten how much fake blood they used. Kato looks untouched. I look like I've been in a gang war. I open a drawer and look for a hair tie. I can at least get that back under control. But I don't find one. The drawers are empty. Clean, white, and vacant. Don't any women live here? Or visit here? Ever? I back out of the bathroom, away from my reflection.

I turn in the hallway and open another set of doors, revealing a home office. This is the first room with color, with warmth. The spines on the books lining shelves at the back of the room catch my eye. Naked wood beams line the overhead like the ceiling has ribs. The desk is made of logs, each corner carved into a swooning angel holding up a thick glass top. The angels' cherub faces are scrunched up. They appear to be in agony. A high-backed leather chair behind the desk faces away from me.

I approach the desk, but nothing on it strikes me as important. It looks like someone is doing taxes. Bank documents and numbers scribbled onto a legal pad litter the surface. Taxes might help the FBI, but they do nothing for my family.

I turn away, but then I do a double take—the chair isn't empty. A sharp yelp escapes my throat. I leap back.

Pressed into the leather chair's green velvet seat and backrest is an older man. He wears an elegant smoking jacket and stares straight ahead toward the bookcases, his face pale white, his fingers on the chair's armrests unmoving. Kato's father?

"Oh no, no, no, no, no," I stammer.

He looks dead.

If I'm caught here, with the head of their family, Kato's father, dead, it'll be worse than having my cover blown. There'll be no coming back from it. I'll be fish food, and my family will be, too.

I reach out to check his pulse. The corpse blinks, and I jump back again.

I breathe a sigh of relief. He isn't dead, but he still doesn't look well. His eyes don't appear to be focused on anything. How can someone this sick be operating his family's tactical maneuvers? How could he be running the siege on my family?

He can't.

Kato's father isn't in charge here at all. Not anymore. He's not picking off my family, hunting us down, making us flee, enacting revenge.

It's Kato.

Kato runs the family now.

I hadn't fallen for the son of the man hunting my loved ones, someone who could be seen as innocent of the crimes.

I had fallen for the person responsible for killing members of my own family.

And I am trapped in his house, cover blown, without backup.

A hand falls on my shoulder. "You weren't supposed to see this. I told you to stay in the foyer." My blood turns cold and all the color rushes out of my face at the sound of Kato's voice whispering in my ear.

RULE 24:

DON'T PICK BATTLES THAT DON'T NEED PICKING.

"Kato," I say, my voice soft. "Is your dad, you know, okay? I mean..." I trail off. Such a stupid question. Obviously, the guy is not okay. "How long has he been like this?"

"Two years," Kato says as his hand slides down from my shoulder to my arm, to my hand, his fingers intertwining with mine. The heat of his body folds around me as he steps closer, pressing himself against my back. "We should go and let him rest." As Kato speaks, his lips are so close, his breath feathers my hair.

I don't fight Kato as he leads me out of the office and closes the door behind us, letting go of me to do so.

"You're the head of your family?" I confirm. *Rule seven: assume nothing.*

Kato nods. "I took over when he got sick. We thought it would only be a couple of weeks, but he kept getting worse and worse. I didn't want you to know yet, since you're on track to take over for your family. I didn't want to complicate things. But I guess I should have known with you here that you'd figure it out. I don't know, maybe deep down I did want you to know."

I haven't gotten used to Kato's Norwegian accent. He stands as stately as a marble statue in the stark-white hallway leading from the back of the house. We approach the sliding doors to the deck. The sun is starting to set over the lake, casting a beautiful deep-red hue against the waves. "I guess neither of us are normal." My eyes stay on Gangster Island in the distance, not daring to look at Kato.

Kato lets out a warm laugh. He takes a step toward me, and I take a step back.

"That's fair," Kato says. "I shouldn't have lied to you. The more people who know that I am the one calling the shots, the more danger I am in. With who your family is, I didn't feel I could risk it. Your family, they think I'm just some in-the-dark, clueless teen born into a bad situation. That's why they never touched me. If they knew who I really was, that I was in charge, they would take me out. I would have to hide here at my house. I don't want that. I know you don't want that for me."

"Of course, I want that for you." My words surprise even me. I turn to Kato. The pain is clear on his face before he wipes it away, leaving an expression that's hard to read. "In fact, I would prefer you in a much smaller cage. Kato, you are going after my family. You are killing the people I love."

"Your *family* are the same people that hit you earlier. Your *family* is a bunch of monsters dressed up to blend in. They are killers. Autumn, you fear those people. I saw what they did to you. And I *see* what they're doing to you now." Kato takes another step forward, and I take another step back, watching his every move.

How had I let myself fall for the target? This is why we have rule twelve: keep your emotions in check. Because you never know when the cute boy you're tailing on a mission may turn out to be the guy taking out your entire family one person at a time.

"Your family wanted to get close to this place to learn its security, yes?"

"Yes." There is no sense in denying it.

"My father never leaves the house. In the past two years, for obvious reasons, but even before that he rarely left. They want to come in here and murder my father in his sleep. Is that what you want?"

"No. It's not your father killing my family."

"They're not your family!" Kato hisses. "They don't behave how families behave!"

"How would you know," I spit back.

Kato takes a minute and composes himself, shoving his anger deep down inside. "You're upset, and I understand that. We've both had a very long and trying day. How about we go to our rooms, take some time, get some space and some rest? We can talk about this again tomorrow morning."

For a moment, I think about his offer, how much I need to get away from him. Then I remember the snipers in the trees lining the drive. He has a lot of manpower. I can't escape, and the longer I stay here the harder it will be to get out. Not to mention, if my family tried to come in after me, not knowing about the snipers, they could walk into a slaughter.

No. I can't stay here. Not even one night. I need to get out.

I give a small humorless laugh. "Kato, you would have to be out of your damn mind to think I would stay here after what I saw. You want my family, including me, dead."

"I don't want you dead. Not anymore."

"Oh, that is so comforting. What every girl wants to hear their boyfriend say." My words drip with sarcasm. This isn't how I imagined missions as a child. This is messy and personal —and snowballing out of my control fast.

"Where will you go if you don't stay here?" Kato asks.

"I'll go back to Gangster Island."

Kato pinches his eyes shut as if in pain and then reopens them after a moment. "I spent the first ten years of my life hiding from your family. I grew up in Norway. When I finally came home to America, I learned all the truths of why I had been sent away. I learned about our families' intertwined history. I would never hurt you, Autumn, but I can't protect you if you go back to Gangster Island."

I shake my head. "This isn't about protecting me. You don't care about that. This is about keeping a high-ranking member of your enemy under your thumb."

"Why would you say that?"

"It's true, isn't it?"

"No, of course it's not true." Something genuine flickers in his eyes, and when he steps closer again, this time I don't step back. I have been trained well enough to identify a lie. He doesn't blink. His body language stays consistent throughout the words. Not a single sign of lying. Kato places his arms around me, resting his hands on the small of my back. He looks at me like I am the prettiest, most precious, thing he has ever seen. "I don't care anymore about a stupid rivalry from the 1960s. What I care about is you and our safety. I need you to believe that."

I nod my head and then bury my face into his soft shirt. I don't want him to see my face. I know he just lied to me. How many other lies have I missed because I haven't been looking for them? Because I have been too caught up in this, whatever this is—or was—with Kato?

I like Kato. A small piece of my heart belongs to him. And it might be the biggest mistake of my life.

Kato takes my gesture as a sign of me trusting him. He wraps his arms around me tighter, holding me closer. I put my arms around him, sliding my hands along his sides, feeling the muscled lines of his waist and lower back.

"It's going to be okay. We're going to be okay," he promises into my ear.

"I know I will be," I whisper back, and I drive my knee up between his legs, hitting him square in the groin. Kato screams and crumples to the floor. I step back, letting him drop. I don't stay to see if he recovers as I dart past him toward the kitchen. I reach the sliding glass door to the deck and am ready to fling it open and run out when I hear Kato cry out. His icy voice stops me in my tracks.

"You lied to me."

I turn around to see him look down at his shirt and then back up at me. Where my face had been buried into his chest, the makeup they put on me at Devils Lake had come off. "You've been playing me. You don't care about me at all."

"Kato, I need to go." My voice is quiet, unsure what else to say. I do care about him—I love him. But if I say that, how will I have the strength to leave? Even after everything he's done, everything he's doing, I still fell in love with him, and love can't be turned off like a switch.

He is the first and only guy I have ever loved. I didn't think it would end like this. I didn't want it to end like this. I wanted us to be able to be together. But I need to go. Even if it hurts. For myself, for my family, I need to go.

"I can't let you leave anymore, Autumn. You know too much."

"You also can't stop me," I say, turning back to the door. I hate how weak my voice sounds. How fragile. I don't want him to know how close I am to tears as I watch his reflection in the glass. It wavers as he stumbles toward me. He is hurting—in more ways than one. If he tries to stop me, I know I can take him. I trust my training. I know I will be strong enough to go through with whatever needs to be done. No matter how much it pains me.

"I don't want to hurt you," Kato calls, this time if it's a lie, I can't tell. I'm not looking right at him, though. I could be missing it. Or wanting so badly for his words to be true I'm not letting myself see it.

"You already have," I whisper.

"You won't make it back to the island if you try to run from me."

"You're going to kill me?"

He isn't carrying a weapon; I checked when we hugged and before I kneed him. Of course, this is his house. I have no doubt he has guns hidden who knows where. And he has men. But they aren't here, and I do have a weapon: me.

"I don't want to, Autumn. Know that. You're pushing me to it. It'd be your fault. You lied to me. You're trying to go back to a bad situation. It's going to get us both killed if I just let you go. I can't do that."

I turn, looking him in the eyes. "In that case, I feel like we should break up." My voice nearly cracks. I need to turn off my emotions. I need to stop feeling this so much.

"What?" Kato stops walking toward me, his face turning into one of confusion. We're in the undefined space between the kitchen and living room. As the sun continues to set, limited light filters in from the glass doors behind me as I stare him down, trying to hide my emotions. Shove it down; wait until I know it's safe. Until he can't see me anymore.

"Did you forget we were dating?"

"No, of course not, it's just—"

"What? You wanted to kill me more when I was labeled as your girlfriend?"

"No!" Kato moves toward me again. "Autumn, please just stay. We can work this all out tomorrow morning when we've both calmed down." He's close enough to touch me. I could fall into his arms, let him catch me. I miss him and I haven't even left yet.

"I love you." It slips out with a tear. What am I doing? Why did I say that? I mean yes, I do feel that way, but not when I know that he could kill me at any second. He's been hunting my family. He's been hurting me and the people I care about. If I stay with him, I will lose everything and everyone. I can't love him. He's a monster.

"Baby," he whispers. His face softens, the stress, the pain, draining out at my words. "I love you too." He holds out his hands towards me. "Come here. Please don't cry."

"I'm sorry." I don't know why I'm apologizing, but everything in me feels like it's shattering. I haven't even known him that long. How can I be this torn up over him? Leaving him feels like tearing out part of my chest and dropping it on the floor. But if I stay, I betray my family, and everyone I love.

Everyone but Kato.

I step forward, collapsing against him. His arms wrap around me and hold me close. I could stay the night, it would be easy to stay with him.

"Nothing is going to hurt you ever again," he whispers to me.

Everything hurts right now. My heart is splintering. I don't want to feel like I constantly need to prove myself. I just want to be me and be loved. I've been trying so hard; I want to be done. I don't want to fight anymore.

"Shh, it's over," Kato whispers. "You can be done fighting." I guess I said that last part out loud. "I'm having a room prepared for you. You can go to bed. Get some sleep. We can talk about everything tomorrow. Nothing has to be decided tonight, okay?"

"I don't want to love you this much."

He holds me a little closer. "It's going to be okay, Autumn. I'm going to take care of you."

At first the words sound sweet. I melt a little more into him, wanting him to hold me, wanting him to protect me. He's going to take care of me.

And then that sensation returns that I had in the car when we got here. I'm not a little kid. I'm not a rescue dog. I am a seventeen-year-old girl. A year shy of adulthood. I am third in line to an empire. I don't need a guy to take care of me. I'm not his charity project. Because I love him, I'm supposed to let him take charge and run things? Screw him. Screw this! What the hell am I doing?

I shove Kato hard in the chest and he lets go of me, stumbling back. I shove him again.

"Hey!" he exclaims, catching my hands as I go to shove him a third time. "What are you doing?"

"I don't know! I am being a total idiot because I love you."

"I love you t—"

"Not the time, Kato!"

"What?"

Confusion wrinkles brow. Does my face mirror his, with his eyes scrunched together, brow knit, and nose perked up to one side? Anger ripples through me. "I'm not some weak little girl." I rip my hands free from his grasp.

"I never said you were," he argues.

I point my finger at him. "I don't need you to take care of me. I don't even know what romantic love is supposed to feel like. It hasn't been that long. I can't even remember your last name!"

He takes a step back, away from me.

God, what kind of a girlfriend am I that I can't even remember what his last name is? Worse, what kind of an operative am I?

I am a whole person without him. I am Autumn Alderidge damn it, and yeah, maybe if I was born in a different family, I wouldn't want to be working in data analysis and building case files, but I want to work with Aunt Magdalena because it's a job I want, and I think would be fun. So, screw settling for the first guy who makes me have butterflies in my stomach. It can't be real love, and it certainly can't be deep enough to sacrifice myself, my morals, and my family.

Especially when I can't remember his last name—when I work for Aunt Magdalena, I plan to write stuff like that down.

"I'm going back to Gangster Island, and you can't stop me."

"Autumn, that would be a mistake." His voice holds a tone of warning.

I shake my head. "Loving you, that was my mistake."

Pain flickers in his eyes before they go back to steel. Emotionless. He rubs the side of his nose with his thumb. "You don't mean that," he says.

Except I do. I mean that, but in a much harsher way. "Just let me go. If you really loved me, you would let me go. You wouldn't hold me against my will."

"Letting you go, will guarantee that I either have to be a shut in, or die."

"Well, Kato, maybe you deserve that. Considering what you're doing, I'd say that would be getting away pretty easy."

I can't leave through the front doors, it's guarded by too many machine guns. I take a step back toward the doors that lead out onto the deck.

"I'm sorry, Autumn," Kato says.

"I'm sorry too. Maybe if you weren't trying to kill my whole family, things could have been different. Also, women aren't pets for you to take in off the streets."

He shakes his head, but it doesn't seem to be in disagreement with what I said.

I shouldn't have left my back to the outside for as long as I do. I realize that a moment too late. The glass doors behind me explode and shatter inward with a crash. I stumble back as shards of glass fall on top of me.

AUTUMN

AGE 6

"Does anything scare you?" I asked, following my father through the gardens, my white winter coat snug around me. My mother had asked me to wear my red one on the property so I wouldn't blend in with the snow. I liked the white one better, though.

My father let out a laugh and dangled his hand out for me to take, which I did, wrapping my tiny fingers around his. Mother kept saying I had the smallest hands for a six-year-old, but my father argued it's a good thing, and he hoped my hands would stay tiny. He said small hands were good for grabbing things in tight spaces.

"I am afraid of a lot of things, Autumn," my father assured me.

"Like what?" I moved closer to him, the path narrowing with the falling snow. I looked up at my father more than anything. My white boots loudly marched along with his silent footsteps. Quinton had told me I could raise the dead with my feet, but I liked how the sound stood out, not yet understanding the danger of it.

"What's your favorite doll in the whole world, Autumn?" he asked.

I scrunched up my nose. "I guess the one Aunt Magdalena sent me from Paris. The one with the big blue bow."

"If someone made a threat to your doll, what would you do?"

"I would hide her away safely in my closet," I answered, proud I'd come up with an answer, but confused by where he was going with this. "Is Quinton planning on taking my doll? What did he tell you?"

"No, my sweet. I'm saying that when you truly care about something, you fear day and night for its safety, whether you hear rumors that there might be trouble or not."

I stayed silent for a moment, pondering his words. My boots bumped the edge of the path, knocking down snow that would need to be cleared. "You're scared that someone may be after us? Me and Mom and Quinton?" I guessed.

"I worry for your safety. I always will. And I will always do what I think is best for you."

RULE 25:

DON'T FALL FOR THE TARGET

I try to get my hands up in time to deflect the jagged glass raining down on me. As shocked as I am, I am beyond grateful it is just me here. If I don't make it back, that's one thing. But, like I would my favorite dolls as a small child, I will protect my family day and night. I may have hesitated earlier, but my mind has cleared, my heart has gotten on board, and even though it hurts like hell, I know Kato and I don't belong together.

My arms freckle with blood as they seep from the cuts from the shards of glass. I slowly raise my head and, as I look up, the glass rain stops. I glare at Kato. He looks unbothered that his entire kitchen is now bathed in destruction. With every slight move, glass falls out of my hair like water out of a fountain.

Something in me changes.

I'm ready to do whatever it takes.

I stand up tall, more glass falling from my head and shoulders. Someone has made a threat to what I care about most, and I must face off against the bully. *He never cared about you*, I tell myself, and my blood boils. *He's been using you. My family will be safe again, once he's dead.*

Hearing the unmistakable sound, I duck, and a knife whizzes over my head.

I turn. A man in camo, like the men along the road leading to the house, is on the deck. A belt full of knives hangs on his hips, and a sneer covers his face like he plans to enjoy this.

Rule twenty-one: don't hesitate.

The man grabs another knife and throws it. This time I'm ready. I reach up, snatching the knife out of the air, but a searing pain burns my hand. I grabbed a fraction of a second too soon. Warm blood drips down my arm, as a lot of curse words come to mind. But it's not the time to show emotions. Plus, now I have a knife. And all it takes is one good blow.

My shoes crunch over the glass as I walk out onto the deck where the man armed with knives waits.

"Don't kill her," Kato orders from behind me. "I just need her unconscious."

How comforting.

The knife man nods, flicking out another blade and lunging at me. He is large and slow, whereas I am small and quick. I drop to the deck to avoid his lunge, but when my hand hits the wood, glass shards dig deeper into my palm and cut. I try not to scream in pain.

The man flings a knife down at me, and I miss a blade to the gut by mere inches. I roll out of the way in time, noting that the knife is left sticking straight up from the polished, wooden surface. In quick succession I sit up, stab the knife I have into the man's thigh, pull it back out to, and grab the knife stuck in the deck, pulling it free. Using strength my wounded hand screams against, I push myself up, knives in both hands. Blood drips down the blade from my injured hand.

Pushing my hair back from my face I feel blood smear against my forehead.

"Now I'm armed. Ho-ho-ho!" I proclaim, parodying my brother's favorite Christmas movie, *Die Hard*. Like John McClane, I won't stop until I win this fight.

The knife man pulls another knife from his belt, throwing it at me while applying pressure with his other hand to the widening blood splotch on his thigh. I dodge the knife and run forward, my own knives out. I slash, aiming for his throat, but he manages to spring back, and all I get is a good chunk of his arm.

The man lets out a howl, but I don't let up. Despite Kato's wishes, this man won't keep me alive. I swing for his face this time.

Knife man grabs my arm, his meaty fingers digging into the flesh as he counters my attack. But, just like my brother had earlier with Kato, I use my immobile arm as a focal point of force and jump up, kicking him with all my might in the center of his chest. He drops me and stumbles back.

I fall to my knees, a knife still in each hand. I really wish I had found a hair tie. I push my hair back again, blood from my hand matting it to my skull. It won't hold for long, but it's something.

I look up—I have won.

The knife man hit his head against the sharp corner of the glass outdoor dining table on his way down, breaking the soft part where the nape of his neck met his skull. Blood stains the deck, dripping from the table like a leaky faucet. He isn't moving. His weight drove him into the table like a hammer hitting a nail. If he's not dead, blood loss will get him soon enough.

Standing tall, I turn my gaze to Kato, who sits at the kitchen counter, watching with mild amusement.

I will protect my family.

I will end this.

Breathing heavily, I'm startled by a flash that catches my eye. Viona drops down from the roof and lands in front of me. She's holding a gun and has it pointed at my chest. "Stand down, Alderidge," Vy orders.

I shake my head. "Well, where have you been? Stand down? Clearly, you don't know me at all, Karen White."

"I know you won't survive a bullet to the chest," Vy responds with a sneer. Like the first time I met her at the roller rink, her lips are bright red, standing out against her pale skin, her face framed by dark locks. She could have played Snow White if crime families ever got together and created a community theater. She had appeared perfect and polished the first time I met her, but now her nail polish is chipped, and her lipstick is smeared against her front teeth.

"That's enough, Karen," Kato calls from inside the house. "I don't want her dead. Just," he pauses, "immobile for a while."

"I can do that." Vy turns the gun's safety on, as if she plans to beat me with it rather than shoot me.

Good.

I can win hand-to-hand combat. Hand-to-bullet, not so much.

Vy and I stand face to face, as if daring each other to make the first move. *Rule twenty-three: let them underestimate you.* I look down at my hand, the one I sliced catching the knife. A large and rather concerning piece of glass sticks out from the wound. I catch Vy's reflection in the glint of the glass as she lunges for me. I drop down at the last possible second.

"Screw it," Vy says, stumbling back from me. She stands next to the knife man—the dead knife man—and flips off the safety on her gun.

I throw the knife in my good hand, my aim sure. Vy jumps to the side, firing her gun wildly. I drop down and tuck and roll through shattered glass, which isn't the smartest move in short sleeves—did I learn nothing from John McClane?—but the quick move does get me away from the line of fire.

I don't need the escape. I watch Vy as she stumbles back, staring down in surprise at the knife in her gut. Then I notice her hand, the one that had been holding a gun. A bullet wound stares back at me from the center of her palm. Kato leans against his kitchen counter, his own gun next to him.

Kato shot her weapon away.

He really doesn't want me dead. The reassurance offers me little comfort. If anything, the thought of him keeping me here alive is more troubling than him killing me.

Vy's hand tightens around the edge of the blade in her gut. When she leaped out of the way, I knew there was only one way she could go, with the knife man's body on her other side.

"Don't pull it out!" I yell, realizing too late what she plans to do. I don't know why I care; she would kill me if given the chance. I don't want her to die, though. I would have happily left had I been able. No one had to die.

Vy ignores me, and I watch in horror as she pulls the knife from her chest, igniting a gush of squirting blood. She falls face first onto the deck, landing on the blade that's in her hand. I don't see where the knife goes, but the pool of blood around her quickly grows.

My gaze goes back into the kitchen. Kato now stands at the doorway that had been blown in. On the floor in front of him, a knife glints in the fading light.

When Kato had rubbed his nose, had he been signaling for the knife man to lob one at my head?

"Are you done, Autumn?" Kato asks, his tone boarding on bored.

I shake my head. "How about you come out here and fight me yourself?"

"I have no intention of hurting you."

"Don't worry, you won't hurt me," I promise. I don't take my eyes off him as I move around the table to where the knife man lays dead. My breath is coming out in heavy pants. I need a moment to pause. I need him to give me that moment.

As I move, I peel the knife out of my injured hand, my skin around the wound rising with the blade handle as my blood had clotted with the blade attached. The wound reopens as bits of my flesh stay fastened on the handle. I swallow back the incredible pain, trying not to let it show.

I need to keep the knife mobile in case I need to throw it.

I am breaking rule eight, but there is just no way around it. *Rule eight: don't leave evidence behind.* My DNA is all over the deck, my fingerprints on the knives. I don't have time for it to be any other way.

"Autumn, please, let's just stop this nonsense," Kato says. "You can take a shower and go to sleep, and we can talk tomorrow. I'll have someone clean this all up. There is nowhere for you to go. The driveway is lined with snipers. The property is fenced. What's the plan here, Autumn?"

My plan so far has been not to die.

"You'll slit my throat in my sleep and ship my remains back to the island long before we can talk tomorrow."

Kato shakes his head. "I told you already, Autumn, that I would never hurt you, even though you lied to me."

"And then two of your people tried to kill me. I think I'm pretty hurt." I drop down next to the knife man, my eyes not leaving Kato as I take the last knife off the man's belt. I hold two knives now in my left hand and one knife in my wounded right.

"That's your fault for fighting. Just put down the knives and come back to me."

"You promise?" I ask.

Kato nods his head. "Autumn, I promise. Please, let's just talk about this."

I soften my eyes, and part my lips, trying to release the tension in my face so I look less like I want to kill him and more like I'm scared. "I don't want to fight you either," I say, making my voice crack, as if I am overcome with emotion.

"I know you've been hurt. I know you're scared. But baby, you need to remember, I am not your family." Kato steps around the glass and blood, skirting the pool of deep red coming from Vy. He makes his way over to me on the deck and

"I was excited when she said she was next in line. You're sure, Abby, that there is no one between her and her parents? I take them out and she gets the throne?"

"That's right," Abby lies.

Why she is lying, though, I'm not sure. Perhaps she isn't on Kato's side.

"Well, that's perfect. If she dies tonight, then I'm almost guaranteed success."

"Ya sure ya want her dead?" Abby questions.

"No, Abby, of course not," Kato snaps. "I want her as an ally. I love her. I want her to rule by my side. Clearly, that's not what she wants. I think a similar situation with her family is what led you to us, yes?"

"Aye. They threw me out shortly after the affair was discovered."

If they don't know about Quinton, I wonder who Abby said she had the fling with.

That's when I notice that I am leaving a cloud of red in the water. Blood is seeping from me. It can't get dark fast enough. If it drifts out from under the dock, Kato and his thugs will know where I am.

For a moment only the lap of the water against the dock can be heard.

"She shouldn't have much air left. She should be surfacing soon," the male voice says from overhead.

"Or she's under the dock," Kato says.

A large splash hits the water. As another large splash hits, I bob I grab the knife from my bleeding mouth and hold my breath as I dive down under the water so I can see whoever jumped in to attack me. Except, the people who joined me aren't alive. It is the bodies of the knife man and Vy, or Karen White. Billows of blood emit from their bodies as weights tied to their ankles pull them down to the bottom of the lake.

I swim to where the bodies are, careful not to move out from the edge of the dock.

My eyes widen. Even in the murky water, it's clear that the knife man and Vy aren't the only bodies at the base of the dock. I let out a gasp of air and push my head up into the air pocket under the dock again, making more noise than I can afford to. I hadn't been standing on rocks. I had been standing on human skulls. I'm breathing faster now; I can hear it. Why am I so loud?

I need to stop; I need to calm down. I've seen dead bodies before. Just not that many all at once.

Bodies in varying stages of decay and rot cover the bottom of the lake. Some have been reduced to just bone, picked clean by the walleyes that haven't been shot. Others have only begun to show the red muscles under their green skin.

Kato has been doing this for a while—and getting away with it. I want to throw up. I clamp my lips shut, trying to only breathe out my nose.

"Did you hear that?" Kato asks above me.

"Hear what?" the male voice asks.

"It sounded like something moving. Below us."

"It was probably the air being released from one of the bodies," the man says.

"Abby, check under the dock," Kato orders.

If I bob back under, I will make even more noise and give myself away. I have no choice but to hope that Abby is on our side and not Kato's. Or, at the very least, that she is on my side. That she cares about me.

I hold the three knives at the ready, one in my injured hand, two in my other hand, hoping I won't have to use them.

I hear Abby moving above me, her feet taking her to the edge before she kneels. A moment later her head appears, upside down, looking right at me, her eyes shining in my direction.

I make no sound. I just stare back at her, waiting. This is the woman who I think of as a sister, the one I have always thought will marry my brother, despite what my parents may think.

The pain of reality hits me, though. She will never marry Quinton. Not anymore. Quinton didn't choose her. Why should she choose us? Why should she choose me?

I continue to bob, waiting in silence.

Abby shakes her head. She's backlit so I can't make out her face. I can't tell what she might be thinking. Her head vanishes back up. "There's nobody down there," she says to Kato, her Scottish accent as thick as ever.

A moment of silence passes again, filling me with dread. If I could see their faces, I could figure out my next plan of action.

"Roman, check under the dock," Kato orders.

Footsteps clatter across the aluminum surface over me. I am so screwed. Abby may help me, but I don't know Roman. No way will he betray Kato for me. I tread backward in the water and keep my movements graceful so I make no sound. I pray I can get back far enough that I won't be visible in the dark and try not to think of the bodies below me.

"I already told ya. There's nobody done there," Abby protests.

"Then you have nothing to fear in letting Roman look," Kato reasons.

I close my eyes as my back hits a cold metal pole. A chill trickles through me. *Please, dear lord, let Roman have bad eyesight.* I am trapped. If I swim out from under the dock, I will be seen by this Roman guy, and he will probably shoot me.

Roman moves again.

"She's down there," Roman says, "but she's unconscious. She doesn't look good, Kato. We leave her down there, she'll die on her own."

I don't think I look that bad. I certainly don't feel that bad. Perhaps some of my makeup hasn't washed off yet in the lake.

Kato gives a deep sigh. "That is very disappointing."

Disappointing? That I was near death? Isn't that what he wanted when he screamed "kill her!" to all his people? I know now he was trying to kill my family, that he was the evil we had been fighting. But wasn't he capable of caring?

"Roman, get Autumn out from under the dock before she drowns herself. Tell the men on the roof to stand down. Get her to her room and get her wounds treated. When she wakes up calmer, we'll talk then. I would lift her out myself but my wrist..." Kato trails off, and I imagine he is showing his wrist to Roman and Abby. A smile comes to my face. Good. *I hope it hurts like hell you bastard.*

Slowly I slip two of the knives below the water and drop them. I can't grip three knives and play unconscious, but I also don't want to give up all my weapons. One. I'll hold on tight to one.

I close my eyes again. Unconscious? I can play "unconscious." If they call everyone else off, that means it's me and Abby against Roman and Kato. That is if Abby will fight with me. It's one thing to tell Kato I'm not under the dock; it's another to fight by my side.

"Abby," Kato says, his voice filled with remorse.

I hear a splash next to me and I close my eyes again, playing unconscious.

"Please," I hear Abby say.

Then a gunshot and another splash. That can't be what I think it is. But as I wait for Roman to come collect my body, I realize it can't be anything else.

Kato killed Abby.

He shot her.

He shot her because of me, and I didn't do anything to stop him.

I should have stayed. I should have gone to bed and talked to him in the morning. If Abby was here then she could have helped me escape. Then she wouldn't be dead. And it wouldn't be my fault. I killed her.

A hand tugs on my arm, pulling me through the water. I can't open my eyes, but I also can't stop the silent tear that leaks from my eye. I hope it blends into my drenched skin. Inside, I know what happened.

A pair of hands grab under my arms and pull me up onto the dock, out of the water. A light lake breeze chills me as I lay there, not daring to move. Not daring to open my eyes.

A gentle hand runs over my cheek. Without opening my eyes, I know it's Kato. I know his touch. He moves my wet hair out of my face with loving hands, and I have to remind myself who he is. What he has done. What he did to Abby. Abby, who knew the rules of our family. Abby, who didn't put up a fight against Kato. Abby, who knows rule sixteen: always have a way out. Abby, who, for as long as I have known her, carries a set of keys to one vehicle or another.

I think about what I saw under the dock. The undersides of two boats, one on each side.

"I love you, Autumn," Kato's soothing voice says. "That's why I have to do this. I am so sorry for what has happened. This is not what I had intended. You know that, though. I know you love me, too. You're mine." Someone pulls at the knife in my hand, but I don't let it go. A pair of fingers then press against my neck, checking for a pulse.

"Rigor mortis?" Kato asks.

Roman makes an I-don't-know sound. Did he no know how to find a pulse?

I don't move a single muscle.

Roman's arms scoop under me, lifting me into the air. As we start to move, I snap my eyes open, spinning in the man's arms, and I drive the knife into Roman's throat with all my strength. He drops me, and I pull the knife out as I fall, keeping my grip on it. I roll off the dock, back into the water with a splash, and I swim toward the edge where Abby would have fallen in.

"AUTUMN!" Kato's voice screams across the lake, and I stop swimming. Someone had to have heard him from Gangster Island. Now they know I'm alive and have escaped. Technically, I finished my mission.

I'm not tired as I surface under the dock and regain my breath. I don't know, though, if it's due to the cold water, the pain, my training, or pure adrenaline.

I go back under, no longer caring as much about how much sound I'm making. He has to know where I am. I just need to be faster.

I look for Abby.

I thought I would find her alive. As I swim over to her, though, the bullet hole through her forehead leaves no hope. I pull Abby back under the dock. As much as I want to, I won't be able to bring her to Gangster Island with me. I have to leave her body here. For now.

"Roman," Kato snaps. "Dammit."

I don't think Roman will survive with that wound to his throat.

Kato calls someone else over to him above me, a new set of feet clanging on the metal deck.

With a silent apology to her, I reach into Abby's pockets, but I find nothing. There are no keys. I discover, though, that she had been wearing a bulletproof vest. She thought Kato would shoot her in the chest if he turned on her. I wish she would have been right.

"Autumn, please talk to me. We have so much to discuss," Kato's voice calls from above, distorted in my ears.

The boat to my left makes a loud grumble as someone turns the motor on. "Shit!" The word slips out as I grab the metal bar under the dock, holding on tight as water is pulled into the spinning blades of the engine. The boat moves away, and the water settles once more, but I feel shaken.

I duck back under the water and pull Abby's jacket off her dead body. My blonde hair will reflect in the moonlight worse than her black jacket. I tie the sleeves over my head, tucking my hair inside, and hide it from view. It is heavy on my head, but I can manage.

I surface under the dock again. I'm going to have to be excellent at counting seconds if I plan to make it home. I can hold my breath for three minutes now before dizziness sets in. But that's in a pool. And on a good day. If I'm being honest, I don't know if I can hold my breath for over a minute right now.

Although my father isn't happy with my speed, I'm able to swim a little over two miles per hour. Quinton isn't much better, so Father lets it slide. Looking across the water, it looks to me to be about a half mile swim to the island. That means I should be able to get there in fifteen minutes. Fifteen minutes of non-stop swimming. I don't know if I can do this, but I don't have a lot of options right now.

I will have to surface fifteen times, meaning fifteen times when I will be a visible target. That is too many times when he has snipers on his roof.

If I miscalculate, I risk staying under too long, and I will have to be above water even longer to catch my breath. I can't let myself get distracted.

I so wish I wasn't working in the field.

"Anything?" Kato yells out toward the water. My guess is he's speaking to the person who replaced Roman and his sucking engine.

I glance down at my feet. I should take my socks and shoes off. They'll slow me down.

I move slowly in the water, reaching my feet up so I can undo the laces.

"Well, keep looking!" Kato calls out. I hadn't heard his foot soldier reply. It could be because the water lapping against the dock is loud in my ears.

I'm careful to drop my shoes so they don't land on Abby, but I know there's no way to avoid all the corpses.

This is it.

I take a deep breath of air and go under, swimming, my legs kicking out behind me, propelling me forward, as I swim underwater.

The water laps toward the island, guiding me as I swim.

Just a short swim.

Thirty seconds in.

Quinton would like this part if he were here with me. He's always liked swimming. He says it clears his mind. It doesn't clear mine. It just makes me tired.

I hear a splash behind me, but I am counting seconds and need to keep my mind focused on that. I can't lose count. I can't.

One minute.

Something grabs my leg and stops me. I break through the surface of the icy lake with a gasp. I twist around and find Kato's eyes staring at me, his dark hair matted around his head as we both breath in the dark night air. He glares. "You need to learn to listen."

"No!" I thrash in the water, but his grip on me is strong. All I manage to do is waste energy I can't afford to waste. "Kato, please."

"I gave you so many chances," he scoffs.

My breath comes in sharp gasps as if a vice squeezes my lungs.

Looking up, I've barely made any progress in my swim. I thought I had gotten farther. I cast a glance over my shoulder. The island is small in the distance. Every light looks to be on, but a guiding light won't keep me from dying. And Kato is right in front of me, clamped onto my leg.

"Why couldn't you just do what I said?" he growled.

"Because I'm not your dog."

I swing my free foot around and into the side of Kato's

head. Kicking again, a straight shot this time into his forehead, I break free and head under the surface. More gunshots ring out and torpedo past me in the water. I alter and shift my direction, and they miss. For now. I swim as fast as I can under the water.

I leave Kato behind me, unconscious for all I know.

I no longer care if he lives or dies. All that matters is getting to the island.

I count again. One minute since my last breath of air. I need to go up. My lungs scream for air. But the fear of those bullets, of Kato catching up to me...

Two minutes since my last breath of air. I can't let my fear result in my passing out in the water. I need air.

I turn over onto my back in the water and stick as little of my face out above the surface as possible to take a deep breath. I can't see anything but the stars over my head, dotting the sky.

Maybe it's for the best that I can't see anything. I'm so tired. I want to be done.

I flip over and go back down. This time, with the evening growing darker, I don't hear any shots.

I do hear a boat motor, though, and I know that if its propellor hits me, I could be hurt. One solid cut and I could die of blood loss. I need to see where it is. I stop swimming and bob out of the water again. The boat stops about where I figure I kicked Kato. I am not as far away from that spot as I would like to be. Someone pulls a body out of the water. I go back under before seeing if the person is okay and continue my swim.

My pace slows as my energy wears out. And I wasn't going that fast to start with. My lungs burn, screaming for air again.

One minute since my last breath. I bob up, gasping to drink in the night. It's hard to stay above the water. I take in a mouth of the lake water and can't get my lips above the surface enough to spit it out. So, I swallow, give a silent prayer that it doesn't make me sick, take a gulp of air, and go back under.

I swim harder. I dig down deep, but there's only so far down you can dig.

One minute since my last breath. I come up again, looking toward the island, and discouragement hits me. Why is it so far? I can't make it that far. But I don't have another option. Except drown. I could always drown. Let the lake have my corpse like it has Abby's. Give in to the inevitable. Stop fighting it.

I go back under.

Fatigue hits my limbs. They like this idea of drowning. I am wounded, and, as I swim—just swim, not fight—the adrenaline wears off.

My hand throbs. My face aches. My toe stings. My head pounds. The water currents brush against my wounds that trail up and down my arms and legs, making them burn as I move. I am losing speed. If I lose much more, I'll be at a standstill.

I pull up for my breath early. I am two-thirds of the way to the island, bobbing in the middle of the southern end of Wisconsin's North Twin Lake. I've lost Abby's jacket, I realize. It's no longer around my head.

A month ago, I never dreamed of being here. And now it's where I may die.

I don't want to die here. I don't want to die at all. I just want to go home.

Fresh pain rips through my arm. I've been hit. I dive back under, silently screaming into the water. I sink closer to the bottom, and though I can't see my arm in the depths of the murky water I know I'm bleeding heavily. It hurts like hell, and the heat of my blood warms the chilled lake water around the wound.

I hadn't seen the gun. I'm hit. And it is real.

God, I want to give up.

I think kicking Kato to the head ruined my last chance of

getting that room he was preparing for me. I don't have a choice. I have to keep going if I want to live. I'm not done yet. Not yet.

I start counting again. I'm not sure how long I have been underwater already. I am slower now with my arm throbbing and turning into dead weight.

I keep reminding myself I'm almost there. It doesn't help as much as I would like.

I have never been more jealous of Ashlynn than at that moment that she gets to be a normal teenager, while I'm in the cold, darkening waters of North Twin Lake. Why can't I be a normal teen with a normal breakup? They get to just say no to Seb when he asks them out. They don't discover that their boyfriend is killing the people they love. They don't have to dodge bullets as they swim for their life.

When I surface, I turn over and once again put my face above the water to suck in a breath of evening air. I don't look around. I know the direction to swim. Any more than the bare minimum makes my body feel like it's casted in cement, ready to sink down and be forgotten. Another victim.

Going back under I paddle as hard as I can, but in my current state I know I'm not going as fast as I should.

I start to feel dizzy.

This has been a terrible plan. I should have stayed and continued to play Kato. My cover had been blown, but so was his. We had both been there, laid bare. Perhaps if I had stayed, I could have found an easier way to escape later.

Or maybe he would have killed me.

I am an Alderidge. I don't know if that holds the weight it once did, but I should be able to leave, to hide, to go to Paris. That will be where I choose to go. I have completed my mission. I always wanted to go and work to get intel on others. I don't want to do field work anymore. This is enough. I can live with that. Assuming I live.

I don't want to be someone else anymore.

My eyelids feel heavy, staying closed longer with each blink. Each stroke I take is like sloshing through a thick syrup. I won't go much farther.

Another breath. Back under.

I don't want my story to end with me drowning in this lake. Maybe they'd still find me. My body could wash up on shore. I could still be saved if I just gave into the darkness dotting my eyes.

Another breath. Back under.

There are worse places to die. At least it's pretty here. Not everyone gets to die where it's pretty. If I float on my back, I could see the stars as I go.

Another breath. I float a little, though I don't let my feet bob up. I could die here. My body is ready to be done.

But if I die, my family won't know the truth about Kato.

Back under.

The black spots in my vision worsen. I don't think I can go any further.

But that's when my hand hits bottom.

I stab the earth with my knife. Using my bad hand, because at least there's not a bullet in it, I pull myself toward shore. The lower half of my body is done. Cool air breezes the top of my head as I wiggle the blade out of the wet earth. I reach forward and stab again. I pull myself out of the water, beaching myself against the shore. Water laps on my lower half, but I don't care. I'm not going to drown.

I made it.

"Autumn," a familiar voice says, and I feel hands, several pairs of them, pulling me onto shore. "Get her father," the voice says.

"Quinton," I whisper, my eyes closing. "Where's Quinton?"

Feet pound the sand around me; I feel the vibrations in the earth beneath me. Shouts and muffled voices filter in and out. I know I'm home.

"We have to strike back!" Ashlynn's voice cuts over the

others as her face appears above me. Fear dots her wide eyes as she takes in the sight of me, and right now I don't have the strength to care. Ashlynn looks over her shoulder. "Look what they did to her!"

Ashlynn is yanked out of my sight, and her muffled protests fade out.

I'm safe.

I made it.

I blink my eyes open, and red hair comes into view above me. My eyes focus enough to see terror on my brother's face. "I shouldn't have let him take you," Quinton says, and he hugs me, knocking air out of me. Everything hurts when he does that, but he's the only person I want touching me right now. I fight to hold on to my consciousness.

"We didn't know," I whisper. "He's the head of his family. It's Kato. Kato is the head. It's all his fault. He killed—" Too many people crowd around. Now is not the time to tell Quinton about Abby.

"How?" Quinton asks, pulling back from me, my body flopping where he doesn't support it. "How did you escape?"

"He underestimated me," I say to my brother.

Harvey moves over my line of sight. He carries a machine gun like he's ready to fire. "Get her inside!" His husband Sam's voice screams from somewhere behind me.

The first pop of gunfire echoes across the lake as strong arms lift me into the air.

The last face I see before passing out is one I haven't seen in years. Worry and concern fill his pinched eyes, closed mouth, and creased eyebrows as he carries me. He's in Spiderman pajamas, something I would have never pictured him wearing. At least, not at our age. Out of his wool coat, though, his muscles are as strong and rippling as any man's.

"Autumn," he says, his Russian accent thick. He yells something in Russian to a person I can't see. The intonation of his accent makes it difficult for me to translate in my hazy state of mind. He lowers his face to mine as we move. "Stay vith me Autumn."

"I thought I could trust him," I say, but my voice hits my ears as a muffled mess. "I thought I loved him. I thought he loved me."

I don't know if Dimitri understands a word I say. Still he answers. "Don't vorry I have you now. It's going to be okay."

I believe him.

And I pass out, looking up at Dimitri Daxterov.

ACKNOWLEDGMENTS

If it weren't for my good friend Autumn Zierman, this book probably wouldn't exist. In one of our many three-hour phone calls, Autumn said to me that a love interest character could never be named Kato. I set out to prove her wrong. Since then, between Autumn and me, this book has lovingly been called The Spite Book, as I wrote it to annoy her—and prove her wrong. Autumn, I love you like a sister, and I win. Haha. :)

Like any book, this one took a village, and I am beyond grateful for my village.

Thank you especially to my wonderfully supportive family, especially Mom (Julie), Dad (Chuck), Reggie, and Claire. I love you guys. Thank you for always having my back, being my beta readers and test audience, helping with edits, and letting me ramble on about my stories always. You guys are amazing!

Huge thank you to Vanessa and Michael at Winding Road Stories for embracing, loving, and supporting this story.

Thank you to all my wonderful friends who have been there for me, including my law expert Autumn Zierman, my child-psychology expert Emma Haugen, my rock Asher Noriega, my morbid expert Jeremiah W. Larson, my sorority big sister Cheyenne Valstar and her adorable dog Nova, Hannah Power, Lucy Nicodemus, Abby Longnaker, Naomi Desai, Diana Tran,

K. Johnson, and so, so, so many others! I am so blessed to have you all in my life.

Thank you to my grandpa, Charles Frederick, who has continued the tradition from his childhood of going to the lake every year for nearly a hundred years. This setting is heavily influenced and set where we have family vacation now. Thank you to my grandma, Clarice, who made the vacation possible when my father and his sisters (Cindy, Cheri, and Lori) were growing up. I am very blessed to have such an amazing family and such amazing traditions.

This book has a lot to do with family, and I want to take a moment to say thank you to those in my family who have left our world but will never be forgotten. Grandpa (Joseph) Foegen, Grandma (Mary) Foegen, Grandma (Clarice) Frederick, Aunt Cheri, Uncle Gary, and John Karsten.

Thank you to Marcia and Brian Freeman for all your advice and support, and thank you to Marcia Freeman and Tony Dierckins for helping me look over contracts and for pointing me in the right directions.

Thank you to Lapshan Fong, Adrian Shirk, Laura Diamond, and all the amazing and supportive faculty at Pratt Institute. Thank you to all the other teachers, too, who helped shape me at St. James, Denfeld High School, and Pratt.

Thank you to everyone who agreed to beta read anything for me, everyone who has given me advice in-studio, and everyone who has helped guide and shape my work. Writing only gets better with feedback. You all prove that again and again.

Thank you to my high school English teacher Mrs. Mickle, who, on graduation night, backstage, before I got my diploma, gave me a hug, and told me she had read my first stage play script and urged me to look more seriously into writing. Thank you for helping to spark that first step, both in your words and by having me write that script for class.

Last, but in no way least, thank you to all writers also suffering from dyslexia, POTS, auditory memory dysfunction, gastroparesis, anxiety, and/or migraines who also came on this journey.

ABOUT THE AUTHOR

Charleigh Frederick is from Duluth, Minnesota, and currently is an undergraduate at Pratt Institute in Brooklyn, New York, pursuing a bachelor's degree in writing. Her works blur the line between good and evil. She also enjoys weaving baskets, obsessing over whatever she is currently reading, and spending time with family and friends.

For more on Charleigh and her work,
visit https://charleighfrederick.wixsite.com/cswrite

Printed in the USA
CPSIA information can be obtained
at www.ICGtesting.com
LVHW041109090924
790521LV00005B/234

9 781960 724021